"SORRY, HOTSHOT." SHE PLUCKED THE CIGARETTE from his fingers. "No smoking, remember?"

"I'm not in a good mood, Marissa."

"Detective, you frighten me."

He ran a finger under her shirt lapel. "You ever do anything with that mouth besides use it to scare men off?"

Her breath caught in her throat as the warmth of his fingers seeped through the cloth of her shirt. He'd thrown her off balance again, and she didn't like it. She'd fix him for that remark. Instead of the comeback he no doubt expected, she asked a question of her own.

"Who's asking?" she said, her voice husky. She laid her fingers on his wrist. "Detective Corelli or Jack Corelli?"

His eyes were dark and hot. Deep, mysterious brown. They raised from contemplation of her mouth to meet her gaze. Slowly, without a word, he shook his head and dropped his hand.

She watched him call for another backup and wondered at her penchant for dangerous things.

WHAT ARE *LOVESWEPT* ROMANCES?

They are stories of true romance and touching emotion. We believe those two very important ingredients are constants in our highly sensual and very believable stories in the LOVE-SWEPT line. Our goal is to give you, the reader, stories of consistently high quality that may sometimes make you laugh, sometimes make you cry, but are always fresh and creative and contain many delightful surprises within their pages.

Most romance fans read an enormous number of books. Those they truly love, they keep. Others may be traded with friends and soon forgotten. We hope that each LOVESWEPT romance will be a treasure—a "keeper." We will always try to publish

LOVE STORIES YOU'LL NEVER FORGET
BY AUTHORS YOU'LL ALWAYS REMEMBER

The Editors

Loveswept® 820

TOO CLOSE FOR COMFORT

EVE GADDY

BANTAM BOOKS
NEW YORK · TORONTO · LONDON · SYDNEY · AUCKLAND

TOO CLOSE FOR COMFORT
A Bantam Book / January 1997

LOVESWEPT *and the wave design are registered trademarks of*
Bantam Books, a division of Bantam Doubleday Dell Publishing Group,
Inc. Registered in U.S. Patent and Trademark Office and elsewhere.

All rights reserved.
Copyright © 1996 by Eve Gaddy.
Cover art copyright © 1996 by Mort Engel Productions.
Floral border by Joyce Kitchell.
No part of this book may be reproduced or transmitted in any
form or by any means, electronic or mechanical,
including photocopying, recording, or by any
information storage and retrieval system, without
permission in writing from the publisher.
For information address: Bantam Books..

If you purchased this book without a cover you should be aware that
this book is stolen property. It was reported as "unsold and
destroyed" to the publisher and neither the author nor the publisher
has received any payment for this "stripped book."

ISBN 0-553-44573-1

Published simultaneously in the United States and Canada

Bantam Books are published by Bantam Books, a division of Bantam
Doubleday Dell Publishing Group, Inc. Its trademark, consisting of the
words "Bantam Books" and the portrayal of a rooster, is Registered in U.S.
Patent and Trademark Office and in other countries. Marca Registrada.
Bantam Books, 1540 Broadway, New York, New York 10036.

PRINTED IN THE UNITED STATES OF AMERICA

OPM   10 9 8 7 6 5 4 3 2 1

For Bob, who never let me give up on my dream

ONE

The mother of all Monday mornings began with a 12:30 A.M. overhead page.

"Dr. Fairfax. Dr. Fairfax to the ER, STAT!"

Marissa Fairfax swore silently, tying off one last blood vessel before she turned to the assisting surgery resident. "Good timing. Close for me, John."

She took the stairs down to the first floor, stripping gloves, cap, and bloodied surgical gown as she went. The chief resident met her at the bottom and told her what he knew about the patient who'd be arriving via ambulance any second.

"There's a gunshot wound to the chest on the way to the ER. Supposed to be in critical condition," Pete Yerber said, handing her a fresh pair of gloves.

"Crazy tonight, and it's not even a Saturday." Thin latex snapped against her wrists as she pulled on the gloves.

"Doing nothing but getting worse too. It's raining like stink and"—he paused as thunder sounded in the distance—"I hear there's a tornado warning."

"Wonderful."

She met the victim as his gurney came flying through the doors leading to the surgical emergency room, gaining her first impressions at virtually a dead run. Spilling details in a spate of words, the paramedic spoke loudly to be heard above the din in the ER. "Blood pressure is eighty over fifty. Heart rate one hundred thirty and respiration is twenty-four per minute. The bullet appears to have entered the chest."

Seconds later they reached Trauma Room One. "One, two, three . . . here we go," Marissa said as the group of doctors, nurses, and techs transferred the patient to the table. Positioning her stethoscope on his chest, she listened briefly. "Breath sounds are diminished on his left side." Not good, she thought. Not good at all.

"Somebody hang some O-negative blood," she snapped, glancing up at one of her residents. "Get an arterial line started and draw blood gases. Put in a central line too." The victim was in bad shape, a fact she didn't have to tell anyone in the trauma room.

"Oh, good, Gina, you're here," she said, spying one of her most promising fourth-year residents. "As soon as the lines are in, you can put in a chest tube."

"Yes, Dr. Fairfax," Gina said breathlessly. "Things are nuts tonight or I would've been here sooner. Is there a full moon? The ER sure looks like it."

"Tornado warning. Same effect." Marissa took the scalpel the resident handed her. "Hurry up with those lines," she told the other resident. "We don't have all night."

An intern appeared with the blood Marissa had ordered. "Man, he's bleeding like hell."

Marissa threw him a quelling look. "We can see that, Conrad. Don't state the obvious. And next time don't stop for coffee." Grimacing, she admitted silently that Conrad was right. This guy was a train wreck if she'd ever seen one.

The patient thrashed around until Marissa placed a restraining hand on his shoulder. "What's your first name?" she asked him in a gentle tone.

"Frankie."

"Okay, Frankie, we need to put a chest tube in so we can drain some of the blood that's making it hard for you to breathe. It looks scary and it's going to hurt, but we can't put you under anesthesia because it affects your breathing. Understand?"

Since she didn't have time to worry about it, she took his grunt as a sign of assent. Quickly, she sliced the scalpel through the wall of his chest. Blood poured out in a thin stream.

"Can't breathe!" Frankie shouted. "I'm dying!"

"You're doing fine, Frankie," Gina told him. "You can't talk if you can't breathe."

Marissa spread the opening with forceps so Gina could plunge the plastic tube into the chest cavity. Frankie screamed, cursed, and screamed again before he lost consciousness. Oh, crap, his blood pressure's dropping, she thought, glancing at the monitor hooked up to the central and arterial vein lines.

Gina sutured the tube in and applied a sterile dressing while Marissa silently ran through a list of possible causes for the patient's loss of consciousness. She didn't like anything she came up with.

"Let's go, people, move it. God, what a mess," she added under her breath.

Another glance at the monitor gave her the patient's vital signs. He was tubing, ready to crash at any moment. If she didn't work quickly she'd lose him. Calmly but rapidly, she continued the diagnosis aloud. "His pressure's dropping and he's got a paradoxical pulse. I think he's developing pericardial tamponade. Probably has a cardiac injury. This one's an elevator case, people, but before we can take him up to the OR, I've got to do a pericardiocentesis."

Though Marissa was outwardly composed, her stomach twisted with nerves and anticipation. As a trauma surgeon she'd had many cases where nothing she did saved her patient, and she hated those cases passionately. Failure, even when unavoidable, ate at her guts. This case wouldn't be one of those. She'd make sure of that.

"Prep his chest," she told Gina, and waited impatiently while the resident swabbed it down with Betadine. Rapidly inserting a long needle to his sternum, she watched red fluid fill the syringe. Immediately she aspirated sixty cc of blood. *Hot damn, I was right. Blood in the pericardial sac.*

The monitors showed sudden improvement in the patient's systemic blood pressure. Exhilaration, intense satisfaction, spiraled through her as the patient slowly regained consciousness. In the span of minutes, death had retreated and life had taken over. Trauma surgery at its best—and most exciting.

Betraying none of those feelings, she spoke calmly. "Get him to the elevator, STAT. He's ready for the OR now."

"Am I gonna die?"

Frightened now that he'd regained consciousness,

Frankie sounded hoarse, faint, and Marissa had to bend over to hear him.

"No, you're going to be fine," she told him. "We're taking you to the operating room right now."

He clutched at her sleeve as they wheeled him out of Trauma One. "Wait. Gotta talk. Wait."

"We don't have time. You're seriously injured. You can talk later."

"Now!" Jerking on her sleeve, he yanked her down so her ear was closer to his mouth. As they rushed to the elevator he started talking incoherently. "Phoenix ring . . . I can give . . . Roth . . . real estate . . . money laundering . . . goes through him . . . land development . . . Roth . . . records . . ."

His pain and the amount of noise in the hallway made most of what she heard unintelligible, and she only half listened. "Phoenix, Roth knows the Phoenix . . . Jerome skimming . . . Let them know . . . he shot me . . . Don't let me die!" Drivel from a critically injured man, she thought. "Jerome skimming . . . from Phoenix."

His fingers suddenly dug into her forearm as he lifted his other hand and pointed a shaking finger. Gaining strength and coherency, he shouted, "That's him! Jerome!"

Following the line of Frankie's trembling hand, she stared at the two men approaching. The uniformed cop left no impression. At first glance she might have dismissed the man beside him too. Medium height, brown hair, physically nondescript, yet he exuded waves of near-tangible malice.

"Bastard!" Frankie screamed. "You'll get yours!

You're dead meat, Jerome! You didn't kill me! I'll live to tell everything, every—"

As if frame by frame, a cold-blooded sequence, Marissa saw Jerome's right arm cross his body, his hand touch the gun at the policeman's hip. Paralyzed, she watched black steel and cold death clear the holster and slash the air, watched fingers squeeze the trigger as the sound of destruction exploded beside her.

Blood—red, glistening, viscous blood. Death running like a river undammed. Frankie . . . *Oh God, it's his.* No operation could save him now. The bullet had drilled its way through the front of his skull to emerge out the back, blowing open that part of his head.

Instinctively, Marissa shut her eyes, her usually cast-iron stomach heaving violently at the sight. Severed body parts and blood gave her no qualms, but naked violence, the slaughter of a human being, burned a horror in her mind. She had watched it happen; she wore his blood and bits of his skin and bone on her clothes, on her skin. A man she had saved from death only minutes before.

Another shot jerked through the sudden silence. Marissa opened her eyes to see the cop hitting the floor. Before she could react to that, the gunman was upon her. Arm around her neck, he choked her, holding the gun to her temple.

"Get back!" he shouted, savagely squeezing her throat. "Anyone comes near me and I swear I'll shoot the bitch."

The gun dropped away from her face. Reacting with a training she hadn't needed in years, Marissa turned her neck into the crook of his arm and sent an elbow jabbing into his solar plexus.

Her attempt at self-defense only infuriated him. "Wanna die, blondie?" The muzzle of the gun pressed close, and she felt the metal whisper of death against her temple.

"No," she said, forcing the word out in a shaking voice. Oh, God, he was going to kill her.

"Good. Then you do like I tell you, and if you're lucky, I'll let you live." He lowered the gun and forced her toward the door that led to the waiting room. "You pigs out there hear me?" he yelled in that direction. "I want a chopper, on the roof, ten minutes. Don't give me no crap that you don't got one, neither."

"Let the woman go, Jerome," someone said. "Let her go, man, it's not worth it."

"Bull. Chopper on the roof or blondie dies." He laughed, sounding gleeful, held the gun to her temple again, and spoke to her. "What did Frankie say to you? What did he tell you?"

Steel ground into her skin; nausea twisted her stomach. She forced herself to answer him. "If you're talking about my patient, he told me that you shot him. That's all he told me. There wasn't time for more."

Her sigh of relief as the pressure left her temple turned into a cry of pain when his fist smashed into her mouth, snapping her head back.

"Liar! I heard him. Enough to know he spilled his lousy guts to you. That little loser gave you everything." Again he slapped her. "Didn't he?"

The copper taste of blood filled her mouth. She felt the skin over her cheekbone split and more blood flow down her face and neck. Staring at him, she realized he was young—mid-twenties at most. But his dark eyes were old—and alive with malevolence.

"Tell me what Frankie spilled and I let you go when we get up to the roof. Don't tell me, and you be dead"—he snapped his fingers in front of her—"like that. Got that?" He wrapped his arm around her neck again and pulled her back against him.

"Yes," she whispered, hating the fear that forced her to obey him. Sweet Lord, she was a dead woman. She couldn't remember a word the man had said. Then she realized it didn't matter, she was as good as dead already.

"Drop the gun, Jerome. Let the doctor go."

Deep, husky baritone, commanding, calm. She recognized that voice, the man. He stood in the doorway, his large frame taking up most of the space, the pistol in his right hand pointed directly at her captor's head.

Corelli. Detective Lieutenant Jack Corelli of the Fort Williams Police. An insufferably arrogant pain in her butt since the day she'd come to Texas to head trauma surgery at Fort Williams Central Hospital. She could have kissed him. If he got her out of this alive, she just might.

"Hey, man, shoot me and she's dead." Jerome's arm jerked and tightened, making Marissa gasp with pain. Hot, fetid breath brushed her cheek. "You can't do nothin' to me."

A smile flickered across the rough features of Corelli's face. "Sure I can, Juju. You know me."

You idiot, she wanted to say, gratitude deserting her instantly. Don't bluff him—oh, God, he's not bluffing, he's going to shoot—don't—

Jerome heaved her into Corelli's arms. A shot rang out as her captor ran out the door of the waiting room.

"Son-of-a-bitch!" Corelli threw her aside and leaped through the open doorway.

"Don't shoot!" Marissa shouted, and dived after him. There were probably fifty people in the hallway. She wasn't about to stand around like an autopsy waiting to happen while desperate criminals and gung-ho cops played shoot-'em-up in the hospital corridor.

She was a pace behind him when he slipped. Attempting to stop, she skidded, crashed into his back, and both of them went down, with Corelli landing on top of her. Two-hundred-plus pounds of solid muscle delivered straight to her diaphragm.

Corelli struggled to sit up, momentarily placing his full weight on her. His voice reached her from a distance; she didn't quite pass out. "Go after him, Edmonds! Call backup! Get the bastard before he takes another hostage.

"Are you all right?" he asked her, leaning over her to feel her pulse. Marissa managed to shake her head. "What hurts? Have you been shot?"

You're the one who killed me, you jerk, she thought, and passed out.

Damn, she caught a bullet, was Jack Corelli's first thought, but a quick inspection proved him wrong. He looked around irritably, wondering why, in a hospital the size of FWC, there was no doctor or nurse rushing to his aid. "Judas Priest, can't somebody help me here?"

One of the people standing frozen against the wall came over and knelt beside him. Yerber, Jack remembered. He knew the chief surgical resident slightly from prior meetings in the ER. "No bullet wound that I could find," Jack told him. "What's wrong with her? Did she faint?"

Yerber patted her down, poking, prodding, apparently checking for entry wounds, even though Jack had already done that. Other than the cuts on her face that were bleeding like hell, she didn't appear injured.

After a minute the doctor looked at him. "Well, I'm not positive, but I think you knocked her out when you landed on top of her."

"What did I slip on?" Glancing around, Jack realized they lay in a pool of blood. "What kind of lousy hospital are you running here that you let blood collect on the floor of the hallway?"

The chief resident met his accusation coolly. "It's your guard's blood, Detective. The cop who let that maniac get hold of his gun lay there and bled while Dr. Fairfax became a hostage. If it hadn't been for the quick thinking of one of our *lousy* hospital's nurses, your cop would have bled out in about five minutes. We haven't had time to clean up the mess."

Jack had the grace to flush. "Sorry," he mumbled. Dammit, he hated it when he was wrong. And more, when he had to admit it. "Will she be all right?"

"She's regaining consciousness now."

"Right. I'll be back. Don't let her out of your sight until I've had a chance to talk to her." Jack rose and limped painfully toward the door at the end of the hallway, praying the backup had picked up Jerome as he fled.

Forty minutes later Jack trailed back into the hospital, his butt dragging lower than a snake's belly. Frankie Lemont's death was a disaster. Two years of work for nothing. They'd been close, so close, and now nothing. Not even the punk who'd shot Frankie. Juju Jerome had disappeared, nearly slitting a nurse's throat as he made his escape.

If he could salvage something in his interview with Dr. Fairfax . . . Jerome suspected she knew something, judging from the conversation Jack had overheard. But the way his luck was running tonight, she'd be in shock from being held hostage. He stopped at the door to the examining room and watched her and Yerber talking.

Even beat up, the split skin over her cheekbone held together by butterfly bandages and the side of her mouth swollen, she was pretty. Jack had never seen her tousled, with her short blond hair looking like she'd just woken up, and fear and pain making her steel-blue eyes huge in her face. He hadn't known she *could* look like that.

Jack's job had sent him to the FWC Emergency Room a number of times, not only in pursuit of criminals but to bring in wounded comrades, most recently his own partner. In the five or six months since she'd joined the staff, Dr. Fairfax and he had tangled almost every time they met. Apparently, she didn't much care for the way Jack did his job.

A self-possessed control junkie. That's how he thought of Dr. Marissa Fairfax. Stubborn, opinionated, bossy, and aggressive—the epitome of the kind of woman he disliked. Professionally, he admired her logical mind, her cool head in a crisis, her assertiveness. On an instinctual, purely male level, however, he couldn't stand her. Marissa Fairfax was as hard, and driven, as they came. And Jack liked his women soft.

This wasn't an ordinary day, though. She'd changed into clean pale blue scrubs, he noticed. He'd have changed, too, if he had a man's brains splattered all over him. No longer the cool professional, at the moment she looked vulnerable. A victim who needed his help.

"Is Dr. Fairfax up to answering a few questions?" he asked Yerber as he stepped inside the treatment room.

Professional replaced victim in a nanosecond. "Dr. Fairfax is perfectly capable of answering for herself," she said. "One of my nurses required extensive emergency surgery, thanks to the criminal who's been running free in the halls of the hospital. I'm going to check on her first. And then I'll have a few things to say to you before I'll consider answering your questions."

Aware that the scorn lacing her voice was at least partially deserved, Jack gritted his teeth. He hated it when cops screwed up. He hated it when anyone screwed up, but especially cops. No way should Jerome have been able to pinch a gun. How he had managed it didn't matter. A suspect should never have been allowed access to a weapon.

"Did you catch him?" she added, staring at him critically.

Scratch hostage-shock theory, he thought. "No. During the, ah, incident with the nurse he managed to get away." She didn't say a word, merely looked at him as if she'd never seen a more incompetent idiot, before turning pointedly away from him. "I'll wait here for you," he said, and watched her walk out of the room.

Yerber laughed, then tried to cover it with a cough. Jack smiled sourly at him. God, he hated it when the cops came out looking bad. Cops were the good guys. They shouldn't lose face.

"Is she really okay?" he felt compelled to ask.

"Says she is." Yerber shrugged. "I'm not about to argue with her. It would take more than a gun held to her head to make Dr. Fairfax break a sweat."

Hero worship, Jack thought, wondering about Dr. Fairfax and her ability to inspire awe. "Yeah, she's a cool customer, all right."

"They don't call her Dr. Ice for nothing," the resident said, and left him alone.

Dr. Ice. Jack smiled at the nickname. It suited her—both her cool, blond beauty and her reserved, professional demeanor. Not for the first time he wondered if the doctor was as icy in bed as she was out of it. Her touch-me-not aura sometimes urged him to find out the answer, but he'd never gone beyond speculation. Tonight especially, professional ethics interfered.

Dr. Marissa Fairfax was a crime victim, possibly a witness in a case he'd been working on for years. He had no business thinking of her in any terms other than professional.

Besides, she wasn't his type.

An hour later, having driven her to the police station, he led her into his office and shut the door. Before he could get a word out, she rounded on him.

"You've given me trouble from the day I met you, Corelli, but even by your standards this latest maneuver—"

"Excuse me, Dr. Fairfax? *I've* given you trouble? *I'm* not the pain in the ass here. The way I remember it, the day we met you did your best to ruin the case I was working on. You were the one who wouldn't let me talk to that suspect when he—"

"That *suspect* was in critical condition!" Her eyes blazed with anger. "He was barely more than a child, not that you seemed to notice. I was protecting my patient, doing my job."

"Bull. You were throwing your weight around. Threatening me with expulsion because I needed to talk to a suspect about his part in shooting a ten-year-old boy. Give me a break, *Doctor.*"

"Give *you* a break?" she shouted. "Why the hell should I?"

Jack gritted his teeth, attempting to take hold of his temper. "We aren't here to discuss our personal opinions of each other. I'm on a case, and I need to take your statement."

"Do you? Fine, but first tell me something, Detective. What gives you the right to place a bet with my life as the stakes?"

Confused, but not about to say so, he stared at her.

"You don't even know what I'm talking about, do you? Of all the arrogant, stupid, criminal—"

She was calling *him* a criminal? "The criminal was the punk holding a gun on you."

"Exactly. Still in the dark? Let me give you a clue. 'Sure I can, Juju. You know me,' " she mimicked, her voice frigid, contemptuous. "You arrogant fool, you would have shot him, wouldn't you? Did it even occur to you that if you had, I'd be dead too?"

His eyebrows lowered, his mouth thinned in anger. "It was a bluff, and it worked. If Jerome had gotten you to the roof, you'd have been dead anyway."

"Dammit, don't you think I realize that? But you were bluffing with my life."

"In my professional assessment of the situation, it was necessary. Sorry I didn't handle things to suit you. Should I have just let the guy kill you without attempting to stop him?" Jack was a good cop and he knew it. His actions had been perfectly reasonable, perfectly defendable.

Silent, she turned her back on him and strode to the window, standing with her arms crossed over her chest and her head bowed. Smooth move, Corelli, he thought. The lady had just been held at gunpoint and he was yelling at her. Some protector he was. He felt like a total jerk.

His voice was too harsh to sound very sympathetic, but he tried. Touching her arm, he said, "I'm sorry I frightened you. And, uh—" He floundered for a moment, then added, "Sorry I yelled at you too. You have a right to be upset." He waited a few seconds, then dropped his hand.

No tears stained her cheeks when she turned to face him. Her back straightened, and he could see the mantle of chilly reserve settle over her like a layer of frost. No anger, no passion haunted the hard blue of her eyes. "Ask your questions, Detective."

The drill began. She might have been discussing a TV show, and a boring one at that, for all the emotion she showed. Jack knew she'd been scared spitless. She was far too smart not to have realized how close she was to dying. How could she be so calm, so collected now? Like ice.

"Was Jerome right? Did Lemont tell you something important?" A long shot, Jack thought, but worth a try.

"Frankie Lemont was critically injured. He babbled. Something about Phoenix and a ring. About Roth knowing Phoenix." Frowning, she added, "Money and real estate and land development. Oh, he said Jerome was skimming Phoenix or skimming from Phoenix. I'm not sure. It was hard to hear and he didn't make much sense at the time."

Not make sense? Holy Mary and all the saints! Frankie Lemont's deathbed confession. Jack's case was back on again, courtesy of the woman sitting in front of him.

"Does this amuse you, Detective?" she asked, her tone dry and irritated.

He'd probably been grinning like he'd just gotten laid. "Not amused, Doctor. Happy. This confession is evidence in a case I've been working on for a long time. I want you to write down everything Lemont said, no matter how unimportant it seems. You understand you'll be called upon to testify in court, don't you?"

"Testify? But you don't have Jerome in custody."

"Not yet. But your testimony in this case will be the deathbed confession Lemont gave you. I'll give you some time to write down what you remember." Now to set the wheels in motion for the arrest of J. Rutgers Roth, real-estate mogul and Jack's key to cracking the Phoenix ring wide open.

Half an hour later Jack walked back into his office to find his witness pacing the floor.

"Here." She slapped a pad of paper into his hand. "Can I go now? How much longer do I have to stay here?"

"Sorry to keep you waiting, Doctor. There's one

more thing to discuss. We need to put you in protective custody. Just until the trial," he added.

"Protective custody?" She gave him a sharp, suspicious look. "What exactly does that entail?"

"Probably the easiest thing would be to find you a safe house. We do it all the time, it's no problem."

"Protective custody means I can't go to work, doesn't it?"

"Well, yeah, you'll have to take off work for a while. For your protection."

"No." She straightened her shoulders and said bluntly, "I won't do it."

"Dr. Fairfax, you don't have a choice. Your life is in danger." But maybe she didn't understand that. Try reason, he told himself. She was a surgeon; she'd understand logic and reason. "This case involves the Phoenix ring. Are you aware of what kind of an organization that is?"

"I read the papers, Lieutenant. Youth gangs, I believe."

"Have a seat," he said, taking one himself. "Phoenix is the organization at the top, controlling several gangs in the area, supplying them with everything from guns to drugs. Frankie was a part of Phoenix. He was this close"—Jack held his thumb and forefinger a scant quarter inch apart—"to giving up the ringleaders. That's why Juju Jerome was told to kill him. And you, Dr. Fairfax, heard Frankie's deathbed confession. A confession that ties J. Rutgers Roth directly to the Phoenix ring."

"Roth?" She frowned and rubbed her forehead. "Didn't I read something about him lately? Some . . . land-development deal or something?"

"Right the first time. Half the rich folks in Fort Williams are involved in Roth's real-estate deals. Frankie told you Roth is laundering money for the organization."

"But no one except you and I know about Frankie's confession."

"Jerome knows it, which means his bosses will know it."

"You're assuming quite a lot, aren't you?" Almost casually, she leaned back, crossing her legs and contemplating him skeptically.

"I'm *assuming* nothing," he said, trying not to grit his teeth. "I'm going on past experience with scum like this. They view you as a threat, so you need to disappear. And even if Jerome's bosses *aren't* worried about you, Jerome is."

"You think he is," she corrected him, "but you have no way of knowing that for sure."

"Frankie Lemont told you Jerome was skimming from Phoenix. Stealing from his bosses. If we find Jerome and put him on trial for Frankie's murder, he's got a chance in the courtroom." Slowly, carefully, so she couldn't help but pay attention, he sat forward and added, "But if you tell a jury in open court what Lemont told you, no lawyer can save Juju Jerome. He's dead. In jail, out of jail, it doesn't matter."

That gave her pause, but she remained stubbornly silent. Jack pressed the advantage. "If you won't do it for yourself, do it for your family. Surely you don't want to put them in danger."

She shook her head. "Sorry, Detective. No family."

Startled, he asked, "None?"

"No one. I'm divorced, childless, parentless. No brothers, sisters, or even a cousin. So you see"—she spread her hands—"Jerome and his bosses have only one thing to threaten me with."

Steepling his fingers over his stomach, he leaned back in his chair and studied her. "Dying is a pretty big threat."

She took a moment before responding. "Understand this, Detective Corelli, I'm needed where I work. My work is important, to me and to others. It's hard enough to live with myself when I lose a patient I've done my best for. How can I live with myself if someone comes into the emergency room needing trauma care and dies because there isn't enough staff to do the work? Dies because I was too frightened to come to the hospital? Because I was hiding out at some safe house?" She shook her head, her gaze steady and determined. "No. That's my final word."

With a reasonable idea of how many people went through that ER in a twenty-four-hour period, Jack knew that head of trauma surgery was no fluff job. Dr. Fairfax was needed, all right, but the hardheaded woman couldn't see that she wouldn't do her patients any good dead.

Her hand was shaking. Not obviously, but when she raised it to brush her hair away from her face, he noticed the trembling. Her face had to hurt like hell. He rose and walked to the water cooler, as much to give himself a chance to manage his temper as to bring her a cup of water and some aspirin.

A smile pulled at her mouth as he dropped the pills into her hand. "Three?"

It just might be the first smile he'd ever seen on her face. He hoped it wasn't the last. He shrugged in answer. "Had my face busted up before. Three work better."

"Thanks." She swallowed the aspirin and stood. "Could someone give me a ride to the hospital? So I can pick up my car?"

"It's at your apartment by now."

Her eyes narrowed. "How did it get there?"

Jack smiled slightly. "The advantages of being a cop. Hospital administration told me where you live. While you were getting patched up a nurse found your keys. One of the other detectives took your car for you. I'll drive you home."

Her gaze hardened. "One of your men drove my car. Without my permission." The dead, quiet sharpness of her voice made it plain she was mad as hell.

Jack frowned. "You were in no shape to be driving."

"In your opinion."

She was a lot more rattled than she let on, he suspected, and didn't like it a bit. "Yes, in my professional opinion. Most people get a little upset when they think they're going to die."

For a minute she stared at him. "I'm not most people."

Jack checked his smile and answered solemnly. "No, I can see that. Forgive me for presuming you might be upset over something as trifling as a hostage situation."

After a moment she relaxed. "Point taken."

"Come on, Dr. Fairfax, let me take you home."

"Suit yourself. I'd ride with Genghis Khan if it meant getting home."

Damn, she had nerve. He liked that. Grinning, he asked, "Meaning I'm a barbarian?"

She pulled the office door open and cast him a speculative look over her shoulder. "You said it, not me. Now that you mention it, though . . ." With that, she walked out the door.

TWO

Marissa slid into the detective's car with a sigh of relief. She didn't know why Corelli had given up on the protective-custody idea, but thank God he had. With no energy left to argue, she wanted nothing more than to be alone when meltdown occurred. Any time now reaction would set in and she had every intention of having a good, long cry. Alone.

Corelli's silence as he pulled out into the street made her wonder if he was more sensitive than she'd given him credit for. Probably not, she thought cynically, remembering his reaction when she'd accused him of gambling with her life. Still, he had apologized—sort of—but more important, she was alive.

Alive. Closing her eyes, she thought about Frankie, who wasn't. Frankie, whose blood and brains and life had been blown out of his head. It could have been her. Her eyes popped open, and desperate to stop thinking of guns and violent death, she focused on the nearest thing. Jack Corelli.

Sneaking a sideways glance at him, she admitted he

was attractive, in a rough sort of way. A blatantly masculine, rugged way. Not precisely handsome, since his
features were too craggy and his nose looked like it had
been broken a time or two. Dark hair, dark brown eyes
that were deep and brooding. Usually autocratic, occa-
sionally crude. Even if some women went for that type,
she didn't.

Still, she couldn't deny that he intrigued her, almost
as much as he antagonized her. She couldn't compart-
mentalize him as she wanted to—he had too many fac-
ets. And that, unfortunately, piqued her curiosity.
Unguarded, unthinking, she said the first thing that
came into her mind.

"Are you married?"

As soon as the words were out, she wanted to kick
herself. Even in the dark car, she knew the look he sent
her held surprise and speculation. She must be in worse
shape than she realized. No doubt he thought the question was her clumsy attempt at a pass.

"No." He sounded amused. "Divorced."

"I don't know why I asked you that." Oh, yes, she
did. Jack Corelli unsettled her, made her feel like an
awkward schoolgirl rather than a competent professional. Something about him, maybe his rampant masculinity, attracted her. Made her contemplate things she
didn't have time for. Things like her neglected sex life.
Why he should provoke such thoughts she didn't know,
but there was no denying he did—and it had happened
before. Nearly every time she'd been around him, unfortunately.

"Don't you?" he asked.

His damnably deep, rough voice didn't help matters
at all. "Small talk, Detective," she said defensively. "It

didn't mean—" She halted, aware she was digging herself a bigger hole.

"Do go on, Doctor. What didn't it mean?"

Her fists clenched in her lap. He sounded so smug, she wanted to pop him. Annoyed with herself and him, not knowing how to answer, she stared out the window. "Anything. It didn't mean anything. Forget it."

"Would you rather talk about Frankie?"

"No!" she blurted out, horrified.

"Relax." He chuckled. "I'm perfectly aware what you were doing. You've held up real well, but there comes a time when it all gets to you. There's no shame in being upset after what happened to you tonight."

Condescending jackass, she thought. "I'm not upset, I'm fine," she stated coldly. "I just want to go home." And crawl into the shower and cry. She clenched her fists tightly to keep her hands from trembling.

"You're in luck, then," he said. "Here we are."

Gratefully, she shoved the door open and hopped out. Before she could thank him for the ride, she realized he was getting out of the car too. "You don't need to come with me."

"Consider it part of the job." The hand he placed under her elbow felt more controlling than supportive, but he did let her lead the way. Once at her apartment door, he plucked the keys out of her hand and unlocked the door.

"What do you think—" She broke off, staring at the gun that had suddenly materialized in his hand.

"Stay put," he told her, and stepped inside.

Marissa hoped that Rosalyn pounced on him. Then she remembered that he might shoot first and ask questions later. "Wait!" she called, charging after him. "Watch out for my—"

She watched as Corelli bypassed the sleek fawn-colored cat meowing at the door, then rapidly checked out her small apartment. A few minutes later he strolled out of her bedroom with a short, "All clear."

He bent to pick up Rosalyn, now winding around his legs, and stroked her fur like a person who knew and liked cats. "Yours, I take it? Not much of an alarm system, is she?"

Watching Rosalyn languidly lash her tail and blink Siamese blue eyes at her, Marissa had to admit she wasn't. "She's a cat, not a watchdog."

"Obviously. Ouch." The cat jumped from his arms, leaving him rubbing the back of his hand. "Sharp-clawed little devil."

"Only when she needs to be."

He raised a brow, but let the comment pass. "Well, I didn't find anything else, but next time wait for me to tell you it's clear."

"Next time?" she repeated blankly, watching him take off his leather sports coat.

"Yeah, next time." He threw the coat over a chair.

"What are you doing?" she demanded, jamming her hands on her hips, confronting him.

"Getting comfortable," he said as he rolled up his shirtsleeves. "Seems like the reasonable thing to do since I'll be staying here."

Her mouth dropped open. "You've cornered the market on gall, Corelli. Get out, right now. You are not staying here."

"Sorry to contradict you, but that's exactly what I'm doing."

"You can't do this to me. Just because I refused to go into protective custody?"

"Sit down," he said, taking a seat on her couch. "You look like you're going to fall down and I can see I'm going to have to explain this to you again. Go on, sit."

His unequivocal assumption of authority tempted her to remain standing just to spite him, but she was afraid she might fall over and prove him right. Choosing a chair, she threw herself into it and scowled at him. "Explain it."

"It's simple. You are a principal witness in a case against J. Rutgers Roth. Roth's case can be a major break for us in the fight against organized crime right here in Fort Williams. *My* major break. I've been working on this thing for a long, long time. If we can get Roth to turn state's evidence, then we can blow Phoenix wide open and put the bosses away for life. And you can link Roth to the organization."

Organized crime. Youth gangs. Good Lord, what had she ever done to deserve getting involved in this mess?

Corelli continued, inexorably. "That means you're in trouble. Since you won't go into protective custody, I have two choices. One of them is to assign you a bodyguard." He lifted a shoulder. "So I did. You're looking at him."

"Well you can just unassign yourself. I don't need a bodyguard."

"Like hell you don't," he shot back. "You're a babe in the woods, Dr. Fairfax. You've got no idea what you're dealing with. No idea of what these people are capable of doing."

A babe in the woods? Marissa tried to remember if anyone had ever called her that before. "Big, bad organized crime?" she asked with a sneer. "Just what do you think goes on in the emergency room? I'm a trauma surgeon, Corelli. Do you think we don't have murderers, drug dealers, junkies, and other scum of the earth passing through all the time?"

"I'm not talking about junkies, or you saving someone's life. I'm talking about Juju Jerome trying to erase you like he did Frankie Lemont. You remember Frankie, don't you?"

Quickly, she closed her eyes and turned her head, her stomach heaving. "Stop it. Just stop it," she whispered.

"You think I'm cruel to remind you, but I'm trying to make you think. This is no game."

"And if I still refuse?" She raised her head to stare at him. Sensing her distress, Rosalyn rubbed against her legs. Marissa reached down to stroke her back, the familiar sound of purring bringing her comfort.

Grim-faced, no inflection in his voice, Corelli said, "Then I turn you over to the FBI."

"The FBI?"

"This case is important, I told you that. The FBI is involved, and if you think I'm a mean SOB, just wait until they get hold of you. If you refuse protective custody, refuse a bodyguard, then they'll make it easy on themselves. They'll slap your fanny in jail as a material witness. And there you'll sit until the trial."

"Put me in jail? For how long?"

"As long as it takes."

"But that could be months." He was bluffing, she told herself. The closed, uncompromising expression

on his face gave her pause, though. He had to be bluffing—didn't he? "I've offered to cooperate. How could
they do that?"

"The FBI will do anything necessary to make sure
you're available when that trial comes up. And so will I.
So, what's it going to be, Doctor? Me or jail?"

Weariness hit her like a gorilla taking up residence
on her back. Suddenly she didn't give a damn what Corelli did or didn't do. She pushed herself out of the
chair, stomped into her bedroom to grab her night
things, then entered the bathroom, slamming the door
behind her. With an audible click, she shot the bolt
home.

"Got an extra blanket?" Corelli called through the
door.

"Go to hell," she muttered, and turned on the taps
full blast.

Jack undid a couple of buttons on his shirt, swung
his legs up, and stretched out on the couch. Closing his
eyes, he laced his hands behind his head and tried to
think about where Jerome might have gone to ground.
He didn't come up with much, and before long he
wasn't thinking about the case at all.

Running water. The sound brought an image to his
mind of Marissa Fairfax standing naked in her shower,
water pouring over her slender body. Though dis-
tracted when he'd landed on top of her earlier that
night, he now pulled the memory from his subcon-
scious. A tempting combination of soft feminine curves
and firm feminine muscles.

He shifted, wishing he hadn't eaten that double

chocolate shake and monster burger for dinner, even though that wasn't exactly where his jeans were fitting too tightly. . . . Cripes, how long could the woman spend in the shower?

He rose and strode to the bathroom, put his ear to the door, and listened. He heard water running and another sound, a muffled sound. Hesitantly, he knocked. "Are you all right?"

No answer. Knocking again, he called out, "Are you okay in there?"

"Go away!"

It dawned on him what was going on. If it had been another woman, he'd have figured it out sooner, but Marissa Fairfax was such a control freak, it had taken him a minute to realize what she was doing in there. Crying, and she didn't want him to hear her. Why did it bother her to cry about something that would have driven most people to hysteria? Or did it just bother her that she might expose a weakness to him—or to any man?

Still, he couldn't blame her for wanting privacy when she broke down, knowing he'd have felt the same. He had to give her credit for the way she'd handled herself with Jerome, and he felt a reluctant admiration for her courage.

Jack returned to the couch, lay down, and closed his eyes. If he had any sense he'd turn her over to the FBI and let them do what they wanted. Except he'd be damned if he'd hand the FBI his case on a platter. They were already more involved than suited him. Besides that, he didn't always have sense, not when someone stirred his sympathy and admiration. Sympathy, my butt, he thought. That icy blonde was stirring up his libido.

Something soft landed on his chest. Opening his eyes, he glanced toward the hallway leading from the bath to the bedroom and caught a glimpse of silky blue above bare legs before they disappeared from his line of vision.

"Thanks," he said, smiling and fingering the blanket she'd thrown to him. He heard the bedroom door slam shut and the lock click. Human after all, he thought. Not to mention incredible legs.

Jack woke to the sound of screams. Instinctively, he grabbed for his gun, rolled off the couch, and hit the ground, running in the direction the screams came from. Her bedroom.

Had Jerome managed to get past the men he'd stationed outside the apartment building? Dammit, she'd locked her door. Thanks to the flimsy lock, the door flew open when he put his shoulder to it. Holding his gun at the ready, he burst into the room.

No Jerome. Marissa sat straight up in bed clutching the sheets to her chest and looking like she would hyperventilate at any moment. Even the placid cat seemed upset, her tail lashing as she stared at him.

"Holy Mother of God," he said, holstering his gun, "you nearly gave me a heart attack. I thought Jerome had gotten in."

Moonlight filtered through a crack in the blinds, enough so he could see her face. Tears shone on her cheeks, her eyes were opened wide, her chest rose and fell rapidly. She must have been having a whopper of a bad dream. Jack took another step forward and hesitated.

"No!" As if to ward someone off, she shoved her arm out in front of her. "Don't—oh, God, don't—"

"Marissa." Speaking sharply, he strode to the bed. "It's a dream. Wake up, you're having a bad dream."

Unseeing, she stared at him, dropping the sheet and clutching aimlessly at the bedclothes. "He's going to kill me, isn't he?"

Jack wasn't sure whether she was asleep or awake. He sat beside her on the bed and gently gripped her arms. "No one's going to kill you, you're safe now." Even though it wasn't exactly true, he figured a lie wouldn't hurt. Right now she needed reassurance more than she needed the truth. He rubbed his hands up and down her arms. God, they felt soft. Soft and silky.

She didn't respond, except to slide her arms around his waist and lay her head on his shoulder. Shocked out of his skin, he sat stone still and waited for her to wake up. Nothing happened, except that she burrowed her head a little deeper into the hollow of his neck and shoulder.

Jack knew how to comfort victims. Knew what to do to ease their fears, to make them feel better, safer, whatever. Ordinarily, though, he hadn't been picturing the victim stark naked only a few hours before. He attempted to move away from her, but she hung on tenaciously, her arms squeezing around him.

Her breasts, bare underneath the silky nightshirt, pressed against his chest. Cursing silently, he put his hands on her shoulders and tried to push her away, and ended up staring at her lips, trembling and unbelievably tempting. Ah, damn, he thought, why fight it? What could one kiss hurt? "Just one," he murmured. Slowly, he lowered his head, intent upon tasting that enticing mouth.

"What—what are you doing?" she asked, blinking.

Her husky voice jerked him back to reality. Holy Mary, what *was* he doing? She was off-limits, she was a victim, she was a job. And he wanted to make her. Bad idea, making it with the witness. He quickly released her and stood.

"You were having a bad dream," he said. "Screaming. I thought—I thought Jerome had gotten to you." He stuffed his hands in his back pockets and averted his eyes.

"You were mistaken." Her voice was cool, crisp, composed. "There's nothing wrong."

Irritated, frustrated, he snapped, "No? Then why were you screaming bloody murder?"

"I wasn't."

He gave up and stalked out the door, slamming it behind him.

The next morning Jack watched the smoke curl from the end of his cigarette and wished he had a cup of coffee to go with it. He caught a glimpse of Marissa's face as she came into the living room a few seconds later, and he wondered what had her all riled up so early in the morning.

Damned if the woman didn't stalk over to him and rip his cigarette clean out of his fingers.

"What the hell do you think you're doing?" he demanded.

"What the hell do you think *you're* doing?" she

countered, crushing the butt out in the saucer on the coffee table. "This is a no-smoking zone, bozo. Blacken your lungs all you want, but not in my home. And take that disgusting thing outside, it stinks."

"Excuse me, Dr. Goebbels. If I'd known I was staying with the cigarette gestapo—"

"Out," she said, and strode into the kitchen.

Not even the inspiring sight of her in a short, silky robe the same color as her eyes curbed his desire to make her pay for that move. "Damned bossy woman," he muttered, but he set the saucer outside on the balcony and strolled into the tiny kitchen. "Don't mind if I do," he said when he saw she was making coffee.

She shot him a dirty look, but added more coffee. "If I realized you smoked, I would have told you last night. It makes no difference to me if you want to kill yourself, but—"

He held up a hand. "Hey, I threw it out. Don't hammer me into the ground, Marissa."

"Who said you could call me Marissa?"

The woman woke up like Attila the Hun. "Considering how cozy we were last night, it seemed reasonable."

"Cozy?" She stared at him blankly.

Jack grinned. "Yeah, cozy. When you plastered yourself up against me."

Her mouth dropped open. Jack had a hard time controlling his laughter.

"Plastered myself—I did no such—" She halted and dragged a hand across her face. "Look, we seem to have gotten off to a bad start this morning. My fault probably. I'm a little . . . grumpy when I wake up. Before I've had my coffee."

"No joke? I hadn't noticed."

She slammed her coffee cup down on the counter and said no more. Jack decided to give her a break. Jerome's handiwork had left her with a black eye and swollen cheek. The sight of the bruises marring her pale skin aroused his protective instincts. "Do you have to work today?"

"No, not until tomorrow at noon."

"Good, maybe you can get some rest. One of my men should be over in a minute to cover for me." He told himself his reluctance to leave was simply because the backup was a rookie, but he had an uneasy feeling that there might be more to it than that.

"Tired of me already, Corelli? Aren't you going to spend twenty-four hours a day with me?"

Briefly, he smiled. "If I do that, I won't get much done on the case. I'll be back this evening. If you want to go anywhere, let Scott know. He'll escort you."

"*I'll* escort me. He can come along for the ride if you insist."

"Fine, I insist." Jack swallowed a healthy gulp of coffee and rubbed the stubble on his jaw. "We're working as fast as we can on this, Marissa. You won't be inconvenienced any longer than necessary."

"Sure. What am I supposed to tell my date tonight?"

"I thought you said you didn't have anyone close that Jerome could get to?" Great, he thought. A boyfriend to get in the way.

"It's a casual date, Corelli. Nothing major."

"Then cancel it. Unless you want a threesome." His mouth kicked up at one corner.

"With you? No, thanks."

"I'm a great date, just ask my ex-wife. Ah, there's Scott now," he said as the doorbell rang. Nevertheless, he drew his gun when he went to the door.

Scott Green, the rookie backup, proved Jack's theory that they were getting cops out of nursery school nowadays. Green didn't bother to hide his pleasure at his newest assignment, either, but Jack didn't hold it against him. He was young, and Marissa Fairfax could have been a sour old crone. It would have been a lot better for Jack if she had been.

"Make sure she doesn't take off alone," he muttered to the rookie. "She's not too thrilled with custody. I've got a feeling she might try to ditch you."

"Yes sir, I'll do my best."

The kid damn near saluted him. "If you remember anything else, give me a call," Jack told Marissa. "See you tonight."

"Be still my heart," she said, saluting him with her cup.

Cheeky, he thought, but he couldn't help smiling. He had a feeling Marissa wouldn't be easy to guard. And Scott, poor sucker, might not last the day.

THREE

Usually, Jack ate lunch at his desk, making do with stale sandwiches and cold hamburgers. When his son called that morning, he figured his workload wasn't so heavy that he couldn't take an hour or so to see him.

Since his car windows were open, Jack heard Tony yelling as he drove up to the house.

"Dad! Hey, Dad!"

A thatch of sandy-colored hair appeared in the second-story window, then Tony hung out of the window, waving at him.

Laughing, Jack pulled into the drive, turned off the car, and got out. "Ready for that burger and fries I promised you?" he called up to his son. No matter how bad his mood, Tony could nearly always pull him out of it.

"Can we go to Burger Busters?"

"Sure, you got it." Jack gave him a thumbs-up sign, hoping Tony wouldn't lose his balance and pitch head-first out the window. Still, Jack thought philosophically, he hadn't done it yet and he'd lived in that house almost his whole life.

"Cool. Be down in a minute."

Leaning against the car, Jack waited, watching the neighborhood activity. Old man Carter raking leaves. The Hollis twins Rollerblading. Sounds of fall, sounds of suburbia. He could never have managed a neighborhood like this on a cop's salary, but Elena didn't have that problem. She'd moved in right after the divorce, using her father's money to buy the house. His child support was pocket change compared with what her old man gave her.

"Come on, Dad, let's go."

Tony climbed into the car quickly, but not before Jack noticed the bruise on his cheek. "What happened this time?" he asked, pointing to the injury as he slid behind the wheel. "That's the second one this month, buddy. What the heck are you doing?" Even an active twelve-year-old shouldn't have that many bruises in a month's time.

"Um, got hit with a soccer ball. You know how it is."

Though he gave Tony a sharp glance, Jack let it pass. "So, I'm glad you called, but what's the occasion? How come you're not in school?"

"Teachers' workday."

"Classes all right this year? Any problems?" Last year Tony had spent a lot of time in the principal's office. As far as Jack knew, this year he was doing better.

"Nah. School's okay." Eagerly, he asked, "Can you come to my soccer game this weekend?"

Jack hated to disappoint Tony, but there was no help for it. "Don't think I can make it, son. I'm on a new case and it's taking up a lot of my time." Nearly all of it, he thought. Funny, but he didn't really mind. Was that because this case related to Phoenix or because of Marissa Fairfax? Jack wasn't sure he wanted to know the answer to that.

"Oh. On Saturday too?" Tony's voice chose that moment to break, making him sound young and sad. "It's just . . . That's okay, Dad, I understand."

Did he? Jack wondered. Or was he just so accustomed to his father missing half of his activities that he rolled with the blows from lack of choice? The familiar pang of guilt crept in. Even without extra duty, his job didn't allow much free time, and he knew his son needed some one-on-one with him desperately. Jack did the best he could, but he often felt he came up short. "Tell you what," he said. "I'll check and see. Maybe I can juggle something and get there for some of it."

"Cool." Visibly brightening, the boy began to talk about his coach.

The smile on Tony's face made it worth anything Jack had to do to get to the game. Maybe he'd take Marissa along if she wasn't working and he couldn't get backup. Do her good to get out and into the sunshine, Jack thought. She was almost too pale to be healthy.

Over lunch, he drew Tony out about school, friends, and his current sport. This was the first time in several weeks Jack had been able to spend some quality time with Tony, and he wanted to make the most of it. It was likely to be a while before he got another chance.

"So, how's your mom?" Not that he gave a flip how Elena was, but whatever affected Tony was important to him. Elena loved her son, but that was about the only good thing he had to say about his ex-wife.

Tony shrugged. Apparently, mother and son were still having trouble getting along. They'd been having problems lately, but Tony wouldn't open up to him about them. Usually, Jack could get him to talk, but not this time.

"She still dating that lawyer?" Jack asked. Tony hadn't said much about the guy, and Jack wondered if that was a good or a bad sign.

"Yeah," Tony mumbled, his mouth full of burger. "Ah-oh," he added, continuing to chew.

"Translate without a full mouth, son."

"He's an a—" At Jack's raised eyebrow, he hesitated and finished: "Butthead."

Jack bit his lip to hide a smile. "Yeah? Why's that?" Not that he disagreed. The times he'd been anywhere near Paxton Welch when the lawyer was at the station with one of his big-money clients, Welch had come off like an arrogant SOB. Why did Tony think that, though? You'd have thought Welch would be nice to the kid if he was dating his mother.

"Thinks he knows everything." Tony's hazel eyes glowed and darkened. "Tells me what to do all the time. Always saying I'm a rude little snot. Things like that."

Well, he had the "little" part wrong, at any rate, Jack thought. The kid had shot up in the last year, and now at nearly thirteen, he approached five-foot-nine. But he was all angles and awkward moves. Endearingly awkward—to Jack, anyway. "What does your mom do about that? Does she let him get away with it or does she tell him to back off?"

Tony lifted one shoulder. "Dunno. Guess she thinks he's right. When he . . . yells at me, she never says much. Besides, she's not always around when he does it." He rubbed his cheek and wouldn't look at his father.

Yelled at him, did he? Jack wondered. The hesitation in Tony's reply had both Jack's antennae and his temper rising. His job included interpreting the difference between what people said and what they really meant. Prudently, he let none of his suspicions show, but when he took Tony home he was going to have a serious discussion with Elena. And she wasn't going to wriggle out of it this time.

She tried to, of course.

"What do you want, Jack? I'm getting ready to go out," his ex-wife said when he finally tracked her to her bedroom.

She was a dark-eyed sexy little beauty, he remembered thinking when they first met. Back then he'd been too sexually attracted to her to realize she had a brain as well, and that she would use her mind and her body to get her way.

Seated on a stool in front of the vanity mirror, her dark hair flowing over her shoulders and wearing only a skimpy black teddy, she was still beautiful. And undoubtedly as hot in bed as she'd ever been, he mused. But sex and looks didn't make up for her lack of other appealing qualities. Elena was his problem only as far as she affected his son, though. She'd lost the power to hurt him in other ways long ago.

"Tony's got another bruise, I noticed. What happened this time?"

"Lord, Jack, you're like a mother hen." Shrugging carelessly, she glanced at his reflection in the mirror and applied her lipstick. "He's a twelve-year-old boy. Somebody opened their locker and he ran into it. Why do you always make a federal case out of everything?"

"Funny." Jack moved closer to stand behind her. "He told me a soccer ball did it."

"Did he? Well, then that's what happened."

The house was silent. A few minutes before, Tony had left for a friend's. Jack and Elena were alone in her bedroom. One of the teddy's straps fell from her shoulder, exposing the creamy top of her breast.

Was it a distraction? he wondered. With the way she flaunted herself around him, he sometimes thought Elena wouldn't be averse to a roll in the sheets again. Or maybe she was just trying to put him at a disadvantage. But lust was the last thing he felt for her. Elena hadn't turned him on in years.

"Last time you said one thing, Tony said another. And the time before that, your stories were different too." His hand fell on her shoulder and turned her to face him. "What's going on, Elena?"

Fear flashed in her eyes, but she jerked out of his grasp and turned back to the mirror. "Nothing. I can't keep track of every little boo-boo the child gets."

Can't bother was more like it, he thought. Digging his hands in his pockets, he backed away a step. "Hear you're still dating that lawyer. Tony doesn't like him much."

"Yes, I've noticed. He acts like a spoiled brat around Paxton. Honestly, it's humiliating for me to have Paxton think I've raised him." Her dark eyes narrowed and she made a moue of disgust in the mirror. "Your influence, I don't doubt."

"That high-society boyfriend of yours wouldn't be

slapping Tony around, now, would he? Because if he is, Elena—"

"Of course he's not!" she said shrilly.

Quick denial, with an overlay of guilt, he thought. Elena's selfishness enabled her to ignore whatever didn't fit in with her desires. Obviously, Welch was one of those desires. But could she ignore signs of her boyfriend beating up on her son?

Hell, yes, Jack decided. "Good," he said. He stepped forward again, taking her arm to pull her to her feet. Keeping a grip on her, he spoke, his voice deliberately dark, packing as much menace as a .357 Magnum. "Because I want you to tell Mr. Paxton Welch something for me. Tell him if I ever find out that he's laid a finger on my son, I'll break every bone in his hands. And then I'll run him in for assault on a minor, child abuse, and every other charge I can come up with. You tell him that." His hand dropped, and he started to leave the room.

She moved swiftly, putting herself between him and the door. "You make me sick, Jack Corelli, Wonder Detective." She was beautiful, her body lush, but her face was contorted with anger. "Don't you threaten Paxton, he's worth a hundred of you. You're just jealous," she hissed, "because you're still nothing but a two-bit cop."

Jack grabbed an arm and jerked her close. "A two-bit cop who can make your boyfriend's life hell if I need to. Make sure I don't need to." He released her.

A nasty smile twisting her lips, she looked at her arm, where the imprint of his fingers showed. "You're still a bully. And a sanctimonious bastard."

"Tell Welch, Elena. I'll be back."

❖━━━━━━❖

By the time he reached the station, Jack had himself under control. His fury hadn't abated, but cold determination had kicked in. First he would find out everything he could about Paxton Welch. Then he'd put the fear of God into the bastard.

Sergeant Gabe Natterhorn was reclining in his chair, his feet propped on his desk, hard at work reading a tattered copy of *Time* magazine.

"Natterhorn," Jack said, passing by on his way to his office, "tear yourself away and run a make on somebody for me."

Without looking up, Natterhorn replied, "Sure. Who is it?"

"Paxton Welch. A CCH, all right? And anything else you can come up with." Not that Jack expected to find much in a complete criminal history of a snake like Welch. The lawyer would be far too careful to have a criminal record. No, they'd find more on Welch by searching the newspapers.

Gabe swung his feet down and straightened. Though he gave an indolent impression, he could do twice the work in half the time it took most people. "That uptown lawyer who's always looking down on us? You think he has something to do with Phoenix?"

"That's the one, and no, it's got nothing to do with Phoenix. I'll be in my office."

"It might take a while."

"Whatever it takes. Just make it thorough." That set in motion, Jack settled down to concentrate on J. Rutgers Roth and the case of the decade.

❖━━━━━━━❖

Marissa opened her door to an unpleasant shock. Instead of Scott, Corelli's darker features stood in her line of vision.

"What are you doing opening the door before I identified myself?" he asked irritably. "Where's Green?"

"Green . . . had to go out. He'll be right back." Uh-oh, she thought, seeing a grim look cover Corelli's face. Scott was a dead duck.

"How did you get rid of him?"

"I didn't," she said defensively, "but I was sure tempted. Have you any idea how annoying it is to have somebody hanging around constantly? I felt like I had a puppy tied to my belt loop. This isn't going to work, Corelli."

"We'll talk about that later. Right now I want to know where Green is."

"Try the parking lot."

He wrenched open the door and started to go out. "The only thing I saw in the parking lot was a couple of kids steaming up the windows. . . ." Stunned, he turned to stare at her. "Green left you so he could go have a quickie in the parking lot?" He stepped back inside, slamming the door shut behind him. "I can't believe this!"

"Watch it, Detective. These apartment houses aren't the sturdiest things."

"Rookies," he said in disgust. "This is what they send me to train. All glands, no sense."

Though she smiled, Marissa felt some sympathy for him. Their jobs were more alike than she'd imagined.

They were both teachers of sorts, and in that capacity, she understood his anger. "You think he met his girl-friend out there? Even if he did, I doubt that's what they're doing, you know. He's only been gone a few minutes."

"That's why they call them quickies. The point is, he left you unguarded."

"What are you going to do to him?"

"Make sure he remembers his mistake," he said grimly. "Before I put his butt on report."

"Corelli—" she began, but he hushed her as a knock sounded on the door.

"Dr. Fairfax, it's Officer Green."

Corelli yanked the door open. Within seconds the rookie was on the floor with his nose smashed into the carpet, his arms behind his back, a gun barrel at his temple, and Corelli's knee digging into his back.

Speaking softly, Corelli said, "If I'd been Jerome, you *and* the witness would be dead. But he'd probably have let you die prettier than he did her. Which you wouldn't have deserved." Releasing Green, he stood and waited while the younger man rose to meet him. "Get down to the station. You're on report."

"But, Lieutenant, if you'll just let me explain—"

"Explain why you decided copping a quickie was more fun than doing your job? Explain why you abandoned the witness and left your post? Get going, Green. And start praying that the least I do is kick you from here to Chicago."

"But . . . but—"

Corelli stopped him with a look and a jerk of his head. Nice trick, Marissa thought, wishing she had it down as pat as that.

With a last despairing look at his superior, Officer Green left.

Marissa contemplated Corelli. "Were you too hard on him?"

"No." He shot her a speculative glance, then looked away. "Too easy, if anything, but I hate it when they screw up like that. He was shaping up to be a decent cop. Now . . ."

"Then don't worry about it. You did what you had to do."

"Yeah?" This time his look was questioning, and not entirely complimentary. "Most women would be telling me I'm a hard-ass and to give him a break."

"I'm not most women," she said, with a faint smile. "I've had to do the same sort of thing with my residents. Sometimes it hurts, but it's part of the job."

"Just part of the job," he said sourly, digging in his shirt pocket.

"Sorry, hotshot." She plucked the cigarette from his fingers. "No smoking, remember?"

"I'm not in a good mood, Marissa."

"Detective, you frighten me."

He ran a finger under her shirt lapel. "You ever do anything with that mouth besides use it to scare men off?"

Her breath caught in her throat as the warmth of his fingers seeped through the cloth of her shirt. He'd thrown her off balance again, and she didn't like it. She'd fix him for that remark. Instead of the comeback he no doubt expected, she asked a question of her own.

"Who's asking?" she said, her voice husky. She laid her fingers on his wrist. "Detective Corelli or Jack Corelli?"

His eyes were dark and hot. Deep, mysterious brown. They raised from contemplation of her mouth to meet her gaze. Slowly, without a word, he shook his head and dropped his hand.

She watched him call for another backup and wondered at her penchant for dangerous things.

Two nights later Corelli dumped his stuff in her apartment. He's like a barbarian staking a claim, she thought.

"What do you think you're doing?" she asked him, motioning to the mound he'd dropped in the middle of her living-room floor.

"Moving in."

"Not in this lifetime, Corelli."

He frowned at her. "Can't you ever just agree to anything? Look, I'm not any happier about it than you are, but this is my case and you're my responsibility. You think I want to stay? You won't even let me smoke here. Hey, get away from that." He broke off to snatch his shaving kit away from Rosalyn, who apparently thought it a likely scratching post. The cat arched her tail disdainfully and stalked off toward the bedroom. "No respect," he muttered before turning back to Marissa. "We're stuck with each other, so why don't you cut us both a break and make the best of it?"

"Make the best of it? Are you nuts? What's good about having somebody I don't even know hanging around me day in and day out?"

"Don't worry, we'll get to know each other real quick. Look at it this way, you're alive and you're working. Isn't that what you wanted?"

"Lucky me." What was the point in arguing with him? She'd do better to hit him on the head with a shovel.

"Ain't it the truth." He pulled a gray sleeping bag from the pile and spread it out. "Your couch sucks. It's got about as much give as concrete. Why don't you have a hideaway bed, like most people?"

Giving in to the urge to provoke him, she said, "The people I *ask* to spend the night don't need one. Uninvited guests deserve to suffer."

"This uninvited guest is protecting your sweet fanny, Doctor. It wouldn't hurt you to be a little more accommodating." Eyes narrowed, he added, "Guess you'll just have to put your love life on hold until this case is over."

That wouldn't be hard, she thought. She hadn't *had* a love life in the last several years. Not that she planned to tell Corelli that. "Guess so," she agreed blandly.

"Got a lot of men friends, Marissa?" His jaw tightened, and he looked displeased.

She eyed him speculatively. "I don't think I owe the police the details of my personal life."

"And I think you do. You told me earlier that you had no one close to you. Now, is that the truth or did you just say it to try to get out of protective custody?"

She knew he'd badger her until she answered. "For the record, *Lieutenant*, I don't have a lot of friends period. Women *or* men."

"That's what I thought." His matter-of-fact tone heightened her irritation. He spread his bag out on the floor. "I'm beat. We can argue more tomorrow." His hands went to the buttons of his shirt, undoing them.

Muscles rippled as he shrugged his shirt off, exposing broad bare shoulders and a rugged chest. Unwillingly fascinated, Marissa stared at the compelling expanse of muscle, her gaze following the dark, curly chest hair that narrowed to a thin line before disappearing into his jeans. Barbarian was right, she thought, eyeing well-developed abdominal muscles and powerful thighs. Her heartbeat accelerated. Heat spread through her veins in a slow, unwelcome journey.

It had been a long time, but she knew what was happening to her. She wanted to curse. Why Corelli? Her response to him wasn't clinical, but coming from a far more personal level. "From where I sit," she said, forcing herself to stop staring at his body, "you're seeing bogeymen where none exist. Juju Jerome hasn't made a move, and I don't think he will. You're dreaming, Corelli, trying to make a big case from nothing."

Sitting on the couch, he pulled off his shoes and tossed them aside. "The hole in Frankie Lemont's head was no dream."

Having no decent response to that, she went to bed.

The day after that, Jack's partner came back to work. Hank Moore had been on sick leave for the previous two months, due to a run-in with a bullet that had narrowly missed taking his life. Jack asked him to guard Marissa when she was at the hospital, figuring that should be light enough duty. With the increased security, he didn't think Jerome could get to her there, but experience bred caution. Even if Hank was still too shaky for full duty, Jack had had enough of trusting rookies and he knew he could count on his partner to take care of her.

That left Jack free to try to get something done at the station. Before he settled in on the Phoenix case, though, he wanted to run through the information Sergeant Natterhorn had gathered on Welch.

"Funny thing, Lieutenant," Gabe said after he brought Jack the file.

"Yeah, what's that?" Jack asked, scanning the report.

"Didn't you tell me this request wasn't connected to Phoenix?"

Jack glanced up. "It's not."

Gabe pointed to one of the sheets. "Take a look at who one of Welch's clients is."

"Client lists aren't supposed . . ." Jack's voice trailed off, and he stared at the paper. Natterhorn had gone above and beyond to get any part of a client list. A mighty impressive client list, too, including some of the most powerful figures in Fort Williams business and society. Holy moly, he thought. There it sat in black-and-white: J. Rutgers Roth.

"Well, I'll be a son-of-a—"

"That any way to greet an old friend?" a voice said from his doorway.

Startled, Jack looked up. A grin swept his face. "Burt King, you old goat, what the hell brings you down this way?"

"Lookin' for trouble, Corelli." The older man walked into the office, glancing around and whistling appreciatively. "You've come up in the world. Who'd have thought the scrawny delinquent would ever make lieutenant?" He winked at Jack and took a seat.

Natterhorn stifled a laugh. "Want me to see what else I can come up with on that matter, Lieutenant?"

"Yeah, do that. Check you later, Gabe."

The sergeant withdrew. Jack stuffed the papers back in the file folder and turned his attention to his old friend. "How's retirement treating you, Burt?"

A rueful laugh shook the former police captain, followed by a fit of coughing. "I get by. Miss the action around here, though. How's the detective business these days?"

Jack lifted a shoulder. "Same old, same old."

"That's not what I hear. Rumors, son. Lots of rumors about you and the Phoenix."

Jack's eyes narrowed. Having worked in the FWPD juvenile division, Burt King had numerous connections. While Jack wasn't surprised that King knew of his efforts, he was disturbed. Somebody was talking who shouldn't be. On the other hand, Jack respected King as much as any cop he'd known. Burt King was the reason Jack had become a cop, and more than that, he was the reason Jack was alive today.

"Cops love rumors, Burt. You know that," Jack said, and changed the subject. Although he wouldn't mind hearing the retired detective's views, he didn't feel right giving anyone beyond his team details of the case. "What brings you here?"

"Took a notion to see you. It's been a long time. Last time we talked you hadn't made lieutenant yet."

"Cut the bull, Burt. What is it?"

King sighed and shifted his considerable bulk in the black vinyl chair. "Word's out on the street that you're close to blowing the Phoenix ring wide open. They're not a bit happy about it. This is big time, Corelli. I'm worried about you."

Jack frowned. "Between you and me, I'm not sure that's accurate. But I'm careful, don't worry."

"I didn't save your skinny sixteen-year-old butt twenty years ago to see you taken out now. Remember that."

"You worry too much, Burt. I know what I'm doing."

"So do *they*," King said, then he let the subject drop. They shot the breeze for a while before King left for an appointment.

A couple of hours later Jack's partner called with the news that Louie, the snitch whose information had led them to Frankie Lemont, was dead. He'd been brought to the hospital with multiple knife wounds and Marissa had taken care of him.

Jack found Hank and Marissa having coffee in the hospital cafeteria. "Thanks, Hank," Jack said to his partner, taking a seat. "The doc here been giving you a hard time?"

"Don't start," Marissa said. "I've been very cooperative."

Jack shot a questioning look at his partner, who merely shrugged in reply.

"See you later, Jack," Hank said. "Captain wants me to follow a lead from the patrol who brought Louie in."

"Right. Don't forget it's your first day back. Take it easy."

"You're worse than my wife, Corelli, and nowhere near as pretty. Good-bye, Marissa."

After he'd left, Jack turned his attention to Marissa. "The admissions clerk says you knew Louie. Says you'd gone to bat for him before, trying to get him off the drugs."

Shrugging, she rubbed the back of her neck. "You

have a thing going with Selma? She's not usually so talkative."

"We go way back," he said, smiling. They'd become friends after Jack had helped Selma's son out of a no-win gang situation a few years earlier. "What do you know about Louie?"

"Not much. He was a POW in Vietnam and a junkie. That's about it."

"You've seen him before?"

"I've seen a lot of junkies before. He's just one of a dozen."

"That's not what Selma said."

She quit rubbing her neck and gave him a dirty look. "That's what *I* say. Can we drop this? I'm due in surgery in a few minutes."

Given no choice, he let it go, but he wondered if she was as unaffected by Louie's death as she seemed.

Late that evening they returned to her apartment together. Marissa went directly to the kitchen. Jack flipped on the TV and sat on the couch. A few minutes later she came into the living room carrying a jelly-jar glass half-filled with a dark amber liquid. Whiskey. He could tell by the smell.

He lifted an eyebrow as he watched her down a hefty swallow. He could be wrong, but she didn't strike him as much of a drinker.

Groaning, she plopped down on the couch beside him and picked up an envelope from the huge stack of mail piled on the coffee table.

"Do you always get so much mail?" he asked curiously.

She frowned and sailed a letter to the floor. "I hate mail. It seems to multiply exponentially while it waits."

"Only if you never go through it," Jack said, a little amused at the quirk. For the life of him, he couldn't figure out how she made jeans and a sweater look so classy. He watched her hands as she deftly sorted through the envelopes. A surgeon's hands, hands that could save a life. They looked almost too delicate to perform the operations he knew she did every day.

His gaze skimmed back up to her face. A swing of pale blonde hair brushed her chin. She was concentrating on her task with apparently single-minded absorption. As far as he could tell, she approached everything that way, whether it was as complex as an operation or as simple as sorting mail. He wondered if she made love as intensely as she did everything else.

Whoa, hold on. Not your business, Corelli, he reminded himself, and tore his gaze from her face. The job, remember the job. Of course, he'd have an easier time of it if she didn't look like an angel made for sin.

"Parties," she muttered in a disgusted tone, and tossed a gilded card onto the floor.

To distract himself, Jack bent to retrieve the card and found himself having to fight the cat for it. After a brief tussle, Rosalyn sent him a frosty glare from unblinking blue eyes, swept up one of the discarded envelopes, and stalked away, her tail held high.

Rosalyn reminded Jack of Marissa. No one did that disdainful look better than Marissa, unless it was her cat. Idly, he glanced at the invite. Paxton Welch was throwing a party. A charity affair held at his very own home.

Jack wanted to laugh. Somebody up there liked him today. What better opportunity to check the guy out? He moved closer to Marissa until their thighs brushed.

There was no reason to feel a jolt at the contact, but he did.

Her gaze dropped to his leg, then raised to look at him.

She wasn't unaware of him, either, and he liked that. Too much, maybe. He held the invitation up to her. "You surprise me, Doc. I didn't peg you as the society type." Another thing he might have been wrong about.

She shrugged. "Notice it was on the floor. No time and even less patience."

"Do you get a lot of these things?"

" 'Tis the season," she said wryly.

Must be, he thought, surveying the rapidly growing reject pile that included, among other things, several invitations. This particular party, though . . . Jack swallowed a grin, imagining Welch's face—and Elena's—if he showed up. One of Elena's major gripes with him had been his lack of interest in furthering her social aspirations.

"Is there any way we could go to this shindig?"

Marissa's eyes widened as she turned to look at him. "Shindig? You want to go to a party with me?"

"Tomorrow night." He waved the invite. "Is that a problem? Can you arrange your schedule so you can go?"

"Probably. If I want to, but I don't." Her eyes narrowed. "I didn't know you had social ambitions. Or are they political?"

"Neither."

She looked at the invitation again, then back at him. "What are you up to, Corelli? Does this have something to do with the case?"

"Maybe. It just might. Tell me, how do you know Welch?"

"We met at a hospital fund-raiser I was roped into going to a few months ago. What does he have to do with Phoenix?"

Jack smiled, but didn't answer her. Shifting, he leaned nearer, feeling a certain tension rising between them. "I've always had a hankering to go to one of these. How about it, Doc?" His voice dropped. "Want to make my dreams come true?"

For a long moment she stared at him. "All right," she said finally, her voice husky.

She could do it, he thought. Make every one of his dreams come true, and he wasn't thinking about parties, either.

When she went to shower, she took another drink with her. It might have boosted his ego if he hadn't seen steam floating from beneath the door. Obviously, she didn't need a cold shower to keep her mind off him. No, just like that first night, she was taking the hottest, steamiest shower she could manage. And that night she'd been emotionally wiped out, though she hadn't let him see it. Was it Louie tonight? Had losing a patient, a junkie, bothered her that much? She sure hadn't acted like it at the time, but then she had her icy reputation to uphold.

The water ran for a long, long time. He'd bet a month's pay that Louie's death was eating at her, and he fought a strong desire to comfort her.

What made him think Marissa Fairfax needed comfort from him? And why did he want to offer it to her so badly?

FOUR

Marissa wondered how long she'd have to endure this party. High-heeled shoes—torture devices invented by a sadistic male—were at the top of her list of undesirable accessories. And if that wasn't bad enough, she had to stand around and make small talk while the damn things grew progressively tighter, threatening to cut off all circulation to her feet if she didn't do something about it. How had Corelli talked her into this?

Glancing around, she looked for a place to sit and massage her poor, tired arches. The glitzy gold-and-white foyer offered nothing beyond a gleaming marble floor, but the huge adjoining living room was liberally sprinkled with Louis XIV chairs and complementary sofas. Welch had a beautiful house, Marissa supposed, if your taste ran to the pompous and pretentious. Hers didn't.

Thank God her dress wasn't as uncomfortable as her shoes, she thought, tugging surreptitiously at the hem. She hadn't worn it in a while and had forgotten that her "classic black dress" was so short, and so . . .

skimpy. Naturally, she'd glanced in the mirror before she left for the party, but primarily to make sure she hadn't forgotten anything. Searching for a pair of earrings had occupied her until she'd heard Corelli telling her to hurry up.

When she'd emerged from her bedroom, the look on his face had reminded her that the dress bared her shoulders and back, as well as a good portion of her chest. His appreciative gaze had lingered on her, giving her an unexpected rush of satisfaction.

But all he'd said was, "Nice."

And dammit, she thought irritably, who would have guessed that Jack Corelli would look like he was born to wear a suit? The conservative navy suit and crisp white shirt didn't mask any of his raw masculinity. At the least, it should have made him look tamer—and less dangerous. Unfortunately, tame was the last word she'd use to describe him.

"Having fun yet?" Corelli asked her, his lips quirking.

She slanted him a scathing look. "Loads. Tell me what you thought—" She stopped when Corelli abruptly looked away. His gaze had fixed on a couple approaching them. Their host she recognized, though not the woman with him.

Startled, she felt Corelli's arm slide around her and his fingers clamp strongly on her waist. "What do you—"

"Marissa," he said in an urgent undertone, "play along with me on this." His eyes, so dark they looked black, blazed with intensity.

The thought came to her that Jack Corelli would be a dangerous man to cross. What was he up to? Curious to find out, she gave a barely perceptible nod and felt some of the tension leave him.

"Jack," the woman said when the two reached them. "It *is* you. I couldn't believe my eyes. What are you doing here?"

He pulled Marissa closer, his hand sliding down until it rested on her hip. A tingle shot through her that she assured herself was irritation. Yet she didn't correct him, or move away.

"Same thing you are, Elena," he said, nodding at the man beside her.

"Oh, I doubt that," the woman said in a petulant tone. "There's not a beer keg in sight."

"Corelli," Welch said. Then he held out his hand to Marissa, saying, "Dr. Fairfax, how are you? So glad you could make it."

"Thank you for the invitation," she responded as she shook his hand. Tall, blond, and slick. Paxton Welch was handsome, Marissa acknowledged, but he always reminded her of a rattlesnake poised to strike. Watching him play the benevolent host, she tried to decide what it was about him that gave her such a negative impression. Perhaps his cold, appraising gaze did it. Or maybe she'd just met her share of men like him and picked up on subliminal messages.

The woman beside Welch—dark, sultry, and very beautiful—gave Jack a smoldering look before she turned her gaze to Marissa. Interesting, Marissa thought, wondering what kind of game she'd managed to get involved in.

"Let me introduce you to Elena Vinciente," Welch said. "Elena, this is Dr. Marissa Fairfax. She's the head of trauma surgery at FWC."

As Marissa nodded she felt Corelli's arm tighten across her back.

After a cursory greeting to Marissa, Elena returned her attention to Corelli. "You're not here on some sort of business, are you, Jack? Surely you haven't tracked any hoodlums to Paxton's doorstep? Stealing hubcaps from the guests' cars, or something like that?"

A slow smile spread across his face. "Not business," he said, his voice deepening. "Strictly pleasure." His hand caressed the curve of Marissa's hip and he turned to look at her.

"Pleasure?" Elena gave a surprised tinkle of laughter. "Jack Corelli enjoying himself at a society fund-raiser?"

"Had an offer I couldn't resist." His expression became blatantly sensual as he smiled at Marissa. "Isn't that right, honey?"

Honey, was it? Marissa stared up at him, wondering what he'd do if she jammed the spike of her heel into his foot. Eyes twinkling as if he knew her thoughts, he gave her a meaningful squeeze.

"Elena," Welch said, before she could answer, "Paige Hunter's trying to get your attention." He turned to Marissa. "Sorry, but we have to run. Duties, you know. Nice to see you again, Dr. Fairfax. Make yourselves at home," he added with a wave. Deftly, he extricated himself and Elena, leading her away rather forcibly, Marissa thought.

Corelli stared after the couple, his expression grim, his mouth stretched in a tight thin line.

"Care to enlighten me, Corelli? And you can take your hand off my butt now. They can't see you anymore."

His hand stopped its lazy stroking motion, and he grinned at her. "Thanks, Doc, you're one in a million."

"The hand, Corelli. Move it or lose it." He let it drop, fortunately for her newly active libido. Oh, God, what would it be like if he made a real pass at her? "Talk."

"Later. Do me a favor."

Her eyes narrowed with suspicion. "Why do I get the feeling I'm not going to like this?"

"If Welch thought you and I were"—his gaze ran up and down her body—"close, it wouldn't break my heart."

"Close. As in an item," she said, wishing the thought didn't send a tingle of excitement up her spine. "What does this have to do with the case?"

"Ever heard of playing a hunch? That's what we're doing here, Doc."

Was it? Or did he have something else on his agenda? "What's the deal with Elena? Old flame? She seemed to know you fairly well."

His mouth twisted into a crooked smile. "She should. We used to be married."

"Oh, for God's sake." Marissa ran a hand through her hair, flicking it away from her face. "You implied this was business. You don't care if Welch thinks we're an item, you want your ex-wife to believe it. Am I part of some jealousy scheme? Maybe I should be flattered, but I can do without it."

He laughed, so easily that she believed his reply. "No, you're my social connection. Relax, Marissa. Elena and I have been happily divorced for years."

For another hour they wandered around, mingling while Marissa's arches fell. If Corelli hadn't kept touching her, it might have been easier to relax. A brush here, a pat there, nothing obvious, but enough to make her more than aware of him. More than aware of the strength—and controlled violence—that lay beneath the smooth lines of his dark suit.

Finally, when her feet ached to the point that she was considering murdering Corelli if they didn't leave, he murmured in her ear, "Help me do one more thing and then we'll go."

One more thing took them on a circuitous route to their host's office.

"Stay there, keep your eyes peeled, and listen," Corelli said, parking her at the door. "This shouldn't take long." Then he opened desk drawers until he found a set of files and started leafing through them, muttering an occasional curse.

"Isn't this an illegal search?" she asked, watching him.

"Yep." Glancing up, he frowned. "Don't watch me, watch the hallway." His gaze fell back to the files. "Amateurs," he muttered.

"You're making me a party to an illegal search?"

"Yep."

She controlled a spurt of laughter at his unequivocal answer. He was definitely bad for her, making her laugh when she should have been mad as fire at him. "Even if you find something, what are you going to do? Steal the file? The evidence won't be admissible, will it?"

"Nope." He shot her a devilish look. "I have this quirk."

"Quirk?"

One shoulder lifted in a casual shrug as he resumed

his search. "A memory-type quirk. If I can read it, I'll remember it."

"What I wouldn't have given for that in medical school," she said with a heartfelt sigh. "But I still don't see what good it does you."

"You don't need to understand," he said with a touch of irritation. "But since I'm such a sweetheart—"

Marissa snorted at that.

Unperturbed, Corelli continued, "I'll tell you. I'm looking for information, not hard evidence."

She peered out the crack of the door. "Looks like you're out of luck. Close it down, someone's coming this way."

He shoved the file back in place and closed the drawer faster than she'd have believed possible. "Come here," he said.

She shut the door and walked toward him. Swiftly he backed her up against the wall, then reached down and grasped her wrists, bringing them up to either side of her face.

Her heartbeat accelerated, sprinting madly. The way he held her, her arms pinioned to the wall, made her feel like a suspect. Vulnerable, defenseless. The sheer size of him added to the feeling. And she'd forgotten the depth of the threat he could exude if he chose. A zing of tension coiled in her belly. "What are you doing?" Her voice sounded breathless, much to her irritation.

Corelli smiled, slow and wicked, and lowered his head.

It must be the fear of discovery, Marissa thought. She had never been the fainting type before, but she felt a distinct wave of dizziness as she watched his mouth descend. His body pressed against hers, he captured her mouth, and his tongue traced the seam of her lips. Shocked by the need setting off explosions inside her, she parted her lips. His tongue swiftly entered, swept her mouth, withdrew, and thrust inside again, this time in a slow, sizzling movement. Hot, hungry, he kissed her as if he had forever. Kissed her as if he wanted—no, *intended*—to make love to her. Almost without thinking, she tangled her tongue with his, kissing him back until he broke the contact.

Still holding her pinned to the wall, he raised his mouth from hers, and their gazes held for a vibrant moment. Then he looked toward the door.

The knob began to turn, and she heard a man's voice say, "What? But I'm—oh, all right. I'll check later." Footsteps clicked on the terrazzo-tile floor of the hallway.

"That was close," she said huskily. "You're crazy to take a chance like this."

"Yeah. Crazy." His deep voice rippled over her, darkly seductive. Motionless, he stared at her, his body crushed hard against hers, heat seeping through their clothes, warming her with a deadly fire. He shook his head. "Absolutely nuts."

This time she braced herself for his kiss, but once again a deep craving overwhelmed her. She'd never realized a kiss could hold that kind of power, could buckle her knees, or make her brain turn to mush.

He let go of her wrists and she put her arms around his neck, driving her fingers into the hair at his nape while his mouth moved over hers. His mouth was firm, and very knowledgeable. His hands fell to her hips, pulling her closer. What was she doing? she thought. A few days ago she hadn't even liked him. But the way he kissed . . . That was something to think about.

Suddenly he lifted his head and released her. "Damn," he muttered. "We've got to get out of here."

Dazed, she stared at him and didn't move.

"Come on, before he comes back." He took her arm and hustled her out of the room, keeping her moving until the next thing she knew they'd said their good-byes and were back in her car.

"You're a fun date, Corelli," she said dryly, regaining her composure and sliding into the driver's seat. "Fasten your seat belt."

"Judas Priest, Marissa, slow down. Who do you think you are, the next Mario Andretti?" The '85 911 Porsche turbo hummed like a son-of-a-bitch, and Marissa was driving like the black hounds of hell were licking at her heels.

"Jacques Villeneuve," she said, flicking him a smile.

Surprised, he asked, "You know racing?"

Downshifting, she sent him a mocking glance. "You could say it's in my blood." Cornering tightly, she put her foot on the gas and shifted up to fourth.

Traveling west on the freeway at one A.M. on a weeknight was a lonely endeavor, thank God. In the blood, she'd said. Nah, it couldn't be. "Mark Fairfax is your father?"

"*Was* my father," she corrected him.

Mark Fairfax, he mused. The world-class race-car driver who'd died in a spectacular crash two years earlier. Since she didn't seem to want it, he gave her no sympathy. "Did he teach you to drive?"

"Drive?" Her husky laugh made him doubly aware of the ache in his groin. "No, Corelli. My father taught me to *race.*"

Gritting his teeth, more from frustration than fear of her driving, he said, "I'd like to make it back to your place in one piece. Try going the speed limit."

She turned a wicked smile on him, stepped on the gas, and shifted into fifth as smoothly as hundred-year-old brandy slides down the throat.

"Arrest me," she told him, her voice dark and inviting. And she hit eighty-five in the next breath.

Jack wanted to strangle her for several reasons, but primarily because she turned him on. He'd forgotten—forgotten, for God's sake—that he was on a job. A kiss shouldn't have been that distracting. *She* shouldn't be that distracting.

Marissa Fairfax was a witness, a job, he repeated to himself for the two hundredth time. Nothing more than that. She was the reason he had Roth in a safe house right now—Roth, his ticket to finding out who ran the Phoenix ring. Anything else, any personal involvement with her, could be an invitation to disaster.

Jack had seen what happened when cops became involved with their witnesses, when they mixed business with pleasure. Loss of objectivity, loss of concentration. The libido took over and good sense waved bye-bye, straight down the tubes. This case was too important for him to screw it up because his hormones wanted to be in charge.

Marissa left the freeway and came to a stop. He watched her legs, encased in sheer black stockings, stretch to operate the pedals; watched her hand caress the smooth knob of the gearshift, lazily holding two hundred and eighty-two straining horses in the palm of her hand. The engine purred its contentment as she eased it into first, then shifted up to the next gear.

He had no business thinking of what she'd look like stripped of that sexy black dress, lying naked underneath him, quivering and straining like that classic engine.

Kissing her had been a major mistake.

Tony perched at the head of the stairs, just out of sight of his mother and her slimeball boyfriend. Why did she like the guy? Even Tony knew the dipwad only wanted one thing from her.

"I can't imagine why Jack was at that party tonight," he heard his mother say.

"That's obvious," Welch said with that smart-ass laugh Tony hated. "But I wouldn't have thought a looker like Marissa Fairfax would hook up with your ex."

"What is it about a blonde that makes men drool?" Elena asked crossly. "She's not that pretty."

Slimeball laughed again. "Marissa Fairfax isn't pretty, she's gorgeous. Not to mention smart and rich. Corelli has the luck of the devil, that's all I can attribute it to. Where's the Scotch?"

"It's about to be poured over your head."

Go, Mom, Tony thought, wishing she'd do it. But then Slimeball might hit his mom—like he'd hit Tony the last two times Tony smarted off to him. The second time, just a few days ago, Tony had threatened to go to his dad. "Do that," Welch had said, "and your father's out of a job. With my connections, nothing would be easier. Believe me, I can do it."

Tony believed him. If he didn't, and Welch *did* get his dad fired, it would be Tony's fault. And his dad would hate him because his dad loved being a cop. No one knew that better than Tony.

"I find jealousy boring, Elena," Dipwad said.

"Then don't come into my house and talk about other women being gorgeous. It's bad enough that Jack's involved with her."

At that statement, Tony craned his head to get a look at his mother. Although she was barely in his line of sight, he could tell by the way she had her mouth screwed up that she was really ticked. His father had a girlfriend? Tony had met a few of his dad's lady friends over the years, but this one sounded new to him. Why hadn't his dad told him about her?

"So what?" Slimeball said. "Why should it matter to you?"

"I don't want him marrying again. Before, I knew there wasn't a chance. The women he dates aren't exactly marriage material. But this one isn't his usual type."

"He'll still pay child support, if that's what you're worried about."

"That's not the main thing. Tony needs him." Elena paused a moment, then continued. "What if he marries her and they start a new family? You know that—"

"Oh, that little technicality you told me about? I thought Corelli found out the truth when the kid was born?"

"He did. The blood tests—"

"I see what it is that's worrying you. You're afraid

blood will win. You think he'll ditch your kid if he has another, because Tony's not his natural son."

"Hush, I don't want Tony to hear. He doesn't know. Jack and I haven't told him."

"The kid's dead to the world."

Tony knew they kept talking, but he didn't hear the words, only the sounds of their voices. Sinking his head in his hands, he tried to make the hall stop spinning, tried not to throw up. His dad had lied to him. His dad . . . wasn't his dad.

The next evening Jack watched Marissa sort through the remainder of her mail pile. Chewing on his pizza, he wondered why she received so many invitations from society types and charity organizations. Even considering that she never went through her mail, he thought the number excessive. Trauma surgeons must make more money than he thought they did. Unless . . .

Jack threw his half-eaten slice of pizza down and stared at her. "Holy—you're loaded. What the hell are you doing living like this and busting your butt in a county hospital emergency room when you've got more money than Ross Perot?"

She didn't deny it, she laughed at him. "Not that much, Corelli."

"What are you playing at? Your old man was rich to begin with, and then to put the icing on the cupcake, he won racing's biggest purse a few months before he died. How could I have forgotten that?" Maybe because other than her Porsche, she didn't live like she was rich, or act like it, either.

"I don't need his conscience money, or want it either."

Surprised by the vehemence in her voice as much as by her choice of words, Jack asked, "Why conscience money?"

"Never mind." She blew him off with a wave of her hand. "I'm a surgeon. What's hard to undertand? Would you quit your job if you were suddenly"—she hesitated a moment—"well-to-do?"

Well-to-do? She was swimming in green. "In a New York minute, sweetheart."

Jack awakened suddenly, heart pumping as he reached for his gun, certain that someone was in the apartment. Blinking, he focused on bare feet and legs, deciding Marissa's foot must have missed his nose by a bare quarter of an inch.

Damn all restless women, he thought. Why'd she have to creep around in the middle of the night and scare the bejeezus out of him? He waited for her to go back to bed, but she didn't do it. A few seconds later strange sounds issued from the kitchen. What in the hell was she doing?

Curiosity drove him to get up and find out. His sleep-deprived brain still couldn't make sense of it, even when he saw her. On a stool with her back to him, Marissa stood on her toes, stretching to reach the top shelf of the cupboard. Baffled, he crossed his arms over his bare chest, leaned against the counter, and watched her.

"What are you doing?" he finally asked.

Startled, she swore and started to fall backward. Jack

stepped forward and caught her against his chest. His intention had been only to steady her, but she was warm and tempting in his arms. Staring down at her, he thought how easy it would be to kiss her, but knew there were reasons he shouldn't. Yet with his arms crossed underneath her soft breasts and her rounded bottom snuggled invitingly against his rapidly hardening flesh, he couldn't remember a one.

"Corelli." She breathed his name like a sigh.

"Yeah?"

"You can let go now."

She had the most incredible mouth. He wanted to feel it open under his, wanted to taste her as he had the night before, and this time he didn't want to stop with a kiss.

"Let go," she repeated.

Her words finally sank in. He released her and took a step backward. Oh, man, she was dangerous. It's a job, Corelli, he reminded himself. A job.

Marissa bent down and started pulling things out from the lower cabinet.

It dawned on him what she was doing. "You're rearranging cabinets in the middle of the night?"

"Looks that way."

"Why?"

"Because I want to." Her voice sounded muffled because she spoke into the open cabinet, down on her hands and knees hauling junk out right and left.

Nice view, he admitted. Damn near perfect, in fact. "Seems kind of"—he searched for the word and finished—"obsessive-compulsive."

Turning her head up to look at him, she blew her hair out of her face and narrowed her eyes. "I'm not obsessive-compulsive. And even if I were to admit that I might be a bit of a perfectionist—"

He choked. "A bit?"

She rose to her feet, parked her hands on her hips, and glared at him. In order for two people to fit in the tiny kitchen, they were forced to stand almost on top of each other. "What of it? This is *my* kitchen, in *my* apartment, and if I want to rearrange *my* cabinets in the middle of the night, I can bloody well *do* it."

"Just an observation," he said, grinning. "Do you have insomnia a lot?"

Marissa returned to her rearranging. "Rosalyn woke me up. She's been acting strange lately. I thought she was sick a few days ago, but then she got over it."

"So take her to the vet."

"If she keeps it up, I will."

"You didn't answer my question," Jack reminded her. He heard her sigh before she spoke.

"When I was a kid I'd wake up all the time to check on my father. He had a habit of disappearing in the middle of the night."

"Bet your mother liked that."

"I don't know, she died when I was two. His girl-friends didn't like it much. Especially since they'd be stuck with me until he decided to come back."

Surprised, he said, "I thought your old man was rich. Why didn't he hire somebody to take care of you?"

"The money came later." She jammed a pot into the corner cupboard. "Look, I don't want to talk about this."

"You brought it up, not me." Why had she? he wondered. Until tonight she'd been about as forthcoming as a brick wall. He knew firsthand what abandonment was like—and it made him feel an uneasy kinship with her. Remembering what she'd told him in the car, he said, "He taught you to race."

"Because it gave his ego a boost. Can we drop it?" Her voice held a vulnerable note.

"Got any cocoa or chocolate?" he asked.

She motioned toward one of the cabinets. "Up there. Why?"

"You need a sleeping aid." He dumped milk into a pan and added the chocolate she handed him.

"Jack Corelli's sure cure for insomnia?" she asked, smiling.

"One of them. If this doesn't work"—he turned his head and let his gaze linger on her mouth—"I've got others."

Her tongue darted out, moistening her lips. She swallowed. "Others?"

He reached out and traced his thumb over her lips. Her breath whispered out, warm, enticing. A man could get into serious trouble with a woman like her. "One in particular comes to mind," he murmured, and replaced his thumb with his mouth. It was a mistake, and he knew it. And he didn't care. Stroking his tongue into her mouth with slow, deliberate thrusts, he put his hands on her soft bottom and brought her snug against his erection.

Her arms wrapped around his neck, her body feeling fluid against his. His hand slipped inside her robe, cupping her silk-covered breast. With a soft moan, she pressed her breast into his palm. He felt her body's surrender and knew he could take her now, standing in her kitchen, before either of them stopped to think.

Jack and the milk reached the boiling point together. The sizzle and splash of milk hitting the burner acted on him like a cold dose of reality. God, he'd been crazy to take her that far, that fast, when he knew he shouldn't be taking her at all.

Abruptly, he let her go and reached for the pan, jerking it from the burner. "Sorry."

"For the kiss? Or for almost burning the milk?"

"The milk," he said wryly. "I think you've got a pretty clear picture of how I felt about kissing you."

Her gaze dropped to the front of his jeans, taking in his arousal still straining against the zipper. She raised her eyes to his and gave him a cheeky smile. "Crystal clear."

He handed her the mug of hot chocolate. "Go to bed, Marissa."

She didn't argue. With a word of thanks, she left.

The next day Jack searched for a logical reason to run a background check on Marissa. It didn't bother him that she was loaded, but if she'd lied about one thing, she could have lied about others. He could see what her job meant to her, but she could have done the same thing in a lot more cushy surroundings. After what she'd told him the night before, and what she hadn't said, he had a feeling her reasons had a lot to do with her father.

The newspapers were a mine of information—at least on Mark Fairfax. Upon his death, Marissa's life became fodder for their mills as well. No surprises. The information was merely a repeat of what she'd already told him, but with more details. Bright, driven, she'd graduated from high school at fifteen and had received her medical degree at a correspondingly young age. Divorced, just as she'd said. Her ex, Gil Harris, was a doctor too. Not as successful as Marissa, by all accounts.

Jack still had work to do on the Phoenix case, and Marissa's background, however interesting, didn't directly relate to it. Natterhorn had taken the information Jack had gleaned from Welch's files and had presented Jack with a file full of the results of his research.

Welch had had financial problems, and they had begun during the savings-and-loan crisis. When a lot of his investments went sour, he'd been left in bad shape. Roth had had his share of trouble too. His downfall had been the real-estate crash. By all rights both men should be dead broke, but neither one was. The opposite, in fact. Both of them had more money than they knew what to do with. They could have made all of that money legitimately, but there was a point when they shouldn't have had a dime. So, Jack wanted to know, where had they found the money to start over?

Roth hadn't spoken a word yet, categorically refusing to turn state's evidence. Either he thought he'd get off or there was something—or someone—who scared him more than going to prison for life. If it had been Jack, he'd have been scared too. Phoenix—the boss, not the organization—couldn't be sure Roth hadn't turned.

Jack believed the FBI safe house was secure, but even so, he had insisted that one of his men guard Roth as well. He didn't intend to lose his key to the case because the FBI got careless.

The phone rang and Jack grabbed it. "Corelli."

"She's gone," Hank said.

FIVE

"Who's gone?" Jack demanded. "Wait a minute, you mean Marissa?"

"Yeah. I'm sorry, Corelli, but she pulled a number on me."

"Where did she go?"

"Not sure. She got a call before she left, some guy named Gil. She didn't seem upset or anything. I went to take a leak and she locks me in the bathroom, shoves a chair under the knob, and ties it to another doorknob. It took me a few minutes to get out. She's in the Porsche, though, so she shouldn't be hard to spot."

Gil, Jack thought. Her ex-husband. Cussing out Hank wouldn't do any good, but he had to tell himself that two or three times before he answered his partner. "We've had a tracer on her line in case Jerome called. I'll find out where the call originated from." He slammed the receiver back into the cradle and cursed.

If he found her safe, he would kill her himself.

Though she was prepared for it, the first sight of her ex-husband shocked Marissa. Gaunt, wasted, his skin sallow, he looked much worse than he had when she'd last seen him, just after he was diagnosed.

"Gil?"

He turned his head on the thin hospital pillow and looked at her. His eyes, the same gorgeous blue, were cloudy with pain. A weak smile spread over his face. "You came. I didn't think you would."

"I nearly didn't." She wouldn't have, if he hadn't made it clear he was dying.

"I'm glad you did. You look wonderful, Marissa. So healthy. And beautiful, as always."

She shrugged his words aside. "Is there really no hope, Gil?"

"You know the odds on pancreatic cancer as well as I do. At least I'm going quickly. Any time now, they said. And I—I can feel it." He smiled wryly. "Come on, Marissa. Look at me."

She did, and she'd seen enough death to know that it looked at her out of Gil's eyes. "I'm sorry."

"Are you? We didn't exactly part on good terms. And you've refused to see me for months now, refused to talk to me."

"There didn't seem to be any point to it. But whatever my feelings about seeing you, that doesn't mean I want you to die." Turning, she started to move away, but he caught her hand.

"Will you ever forgive me?"

She pulled her hand from his. "For what? The lying? The affair?"

"I hurt you. I didn't want to. Didn't intend to."

She looked at him. For so long she hadn't believed

that. Her bitterness intact, she'd been sure that Gil had used her and hadn't given a damn what he'd done to her life. His explanations, his excuses, hadn't moved her. But now he was dying. And she knew, deep down, that he wasn't a bad man. Yet it still hurt.

"If you didn't want to hurt me," she asked, "why the *hell* did you marry me when you must have known you were gay?"

"Because I couldn't admit it, I wanted so badly not to be. And you were beautiful, successful, everything I should have wanted."

"Except for one minor detail," she said dryly. "I'm a woman."

"Marissa, let me—"

"When I found out you were having an affair, I felt like a fool. Another woman I could have fought, but a man?" She shook her head. "For months I told myself that our problems were due to my career."

"That was part of it," he admitted. "Your career was taking off and mine was stalled. You were a rising star and I was nothing special. But my jealousy of your career was a handy excuse to mask the real problem." He paused. "You still hate me, don't you?"

She didn't respond, unsure what she wanted to say, or even why she was there. Maybe because she wasn't a coward, and she had to prove that to herself by facing the past. Finally, she answered him. "For a long time I did hate you. Now—I'm not sure what I feel. I want to let go of the anger. Anger sours after holding on to it for years."

"Why didn't you marry Rodgers?"

"Marry Larry Rodgers?" She smiled, remembering Larry fondly. A friend, then a lover, and now a friend again. "No, that wouldn't have worked. But he helped me through a rough time." The time right after the divorce had been the worst. Larry had made it bearable.

"I'm glad he was there for you."

"What's this about, Gil? Are you asking for absolution?" She crossed her arms over her stomach. Had she truly been in love with Gil? When she married him she'd thought so.

"Not absolution." Weakly, he shook his head. "Just to know that I didn't destroy your life."

"I won't deny that it hurt, but it didn't destroy me. I found out I was stronger than I knew." And not nearly as naive as she'd been. She knew better now than to blame herself for someone else's choices.

"We were friends before we married. Good friends. Could we—" He broke off. "No, I've no right to ask you."

"No, you don't." Her neck ached; she rubbed it and thought about what he'd said. Forgiveness. Not for Gil's sake so much as her own. "You know me, Gil. You knew how hard I'd find it to turn down a deathbed request. The minute you said you were dying, you knew I'd come."

"It wasn't fair, I know. But I don't have time to be fair, Marissa. I am dying, and I wanted to make it right before I go. You've refused to see me so many times, I had to use the only thing I had to get you to come. I want to make peace now. Is there any way I can do that?"

"You really didn't know when we married, did you?" At first she'd been sure he'd known and had deliberately used her, but maybe she'd been wrong. Back then she hadn't *wanted* to know Gil's side of things.

He turned his face to the wall. Softly, he said, "No, I didn't know. I refused to allow it, refused to let myself even consider the possibility that I was gay. It took me a long time to realize I was living a lie and forcing you to live it too. You deserved better than that."

Marissa couldn't absolve him from blame, she couldn't be his friend again. But there was one thing she could do, for both of them. Let go of the bitterness and allow him to die a little easier.

"Stay for a while?" he asked, his voice fading. He held out his hand.

Hesitantly, she placed hers in his.

"Thank you," he whispered.

She sat beside him, watching as he fell asleep and thinking as afternoon slipped into twilight.

Marissa jumped as high as a cat on catnip when he touched her. Jack tightened his grip on her arms and smiled grimly. "Surprised to see me?" he asked, his tone soft, slick, and dangerous.

The drive to Houston and the long wait in the chill drizzling rain outside M. D. Anderson Hospital had given Jack's anger plenty of time to simmer. When he finally saw Marissa stroll out of the hospital into the gloom-ridden twilight, his wrath had exploded in a full, rolling boil.

"What—what are you doing here?" She blinked at him as if she wasn't quite sure where she was.

"Chasing after you. You're supposed to be in protective custody, remember? Then you decide to slip your leash. What the hell are you playing at?"

Her face flushed, anger burned in her eyes. "Let go of me. And stop shouting at me."

"You think this is shouting? Honey, I'm just getting warmed up. My day started in the garbage can and it's gone downhill from there. You better have a damned good reason why you locked my partner in the john and hightailed it to Houston."

Squirming, she tried to break his grip, but he wasn't about to loosen his hold. When she realized the futility of fighting, she stilled, but she didn't back down. Her stubborn chin came up as she said, "I'm not going to tell you one damned thing. You're a detective. Detect."

Jack jerked her close to him. Anger deepened his voice, roughened it, so it emerged as a harsh, rusty bass. "What I'd like to figure out"—he curved one hand around her throat—"is how to strangle you and get away with it. But since I wouldn't have a material witness then, I guess this is your lucky day. Now, what were you doing?"

She raised her hand and knocked his away. He slid it down her shoulder to her arm and gripped both of her arms again, his fingers digging into her flesh through the light jacket she wore. Jack knew her flight had been a spur-of-the-moment decision, but that didn't make him any more sympathetic. He was too damned mad to waste any sympathy on her.

That cool, frosty look came into her eyes again. "Personal business, Lieutenant. *Private*, personal business."

"So private and personal you had to risk getting killed?"

"What risk?" She glanced around at the people milling about in the twilight. "I don't see any killers, do you? Just a bunch of ordinary folks going home to dinner. Super cop strikes out. You can't admit when you're wrong, can you, Corelli?"

He slid one hand to the small of her back and pulled her flush against him. His other hand slipped through the pale silk of her hair to the back of her head, holding her so their faces were inches apart. Her tongue was sharp, but her mouth—God, her mouth looked soft and seductive. Her heartbeat, and his, sped up, beating together in erratic unison. In the middle of a crowded Houston sidewalk surrounded by people, he saw only her, was aware only of her.

"A mouth like yours shouldn't be wasted on flaying a man, Marissa," he murmured. "A mouth like yours is made for better things." She was pure temptation, wrapped up in an icy coating that he wanted to melt, and then watch her go up in flames. "You're not playing with fire, baby, you're trifling with pure nitro."

He wanted to frighten her, to throw her off balance, to make her back off before he made the ultimate mistake. But he should have known her better. He *did* know her better. Jack doubted Marissa Fairfax had ever backed away from a confrontation in her life.

"I've always liked a challenge," she said huskily, her face lifted to his, daring him.

He'd never had a better offer, or a more inflammatory one. Their lips met at the same moment he heard a low-pitched whine and then the ping of the ricochet. He shoved her to the sidewalk and followed her down, shielding her with his body.

"Are you crazy?" she shouted, squirming underneath him. "Get off!"

"Shut up." He flinched as a second bullet creased

the fleshy part of his upper arm. Damn, he'd forgotten how much a flesh wound stung.

"Don't you—"

He cut her off by slapping his palm over her mouth. Drawing his gun with his other hand, he cautiously raised his head. People stared at them curiously as they walked by, but since the shooter had used a silencer, no one knew exactly what they were doing. In the way of big cities, no one really cared. In fact, most people gave them an even wider berth when they got an eyeful of Jack's gun.

By the time a few minutes had passed, Jack knew the sniper had fled. Not that he could have risked a shot anyway, with all the pedestrians milling around.

"Dammit!" He rolled off Marissa and rose, swearing again fluently. His hand clamped on her arm, jerking her roughly to her feet.

"What's the matter with you?" Her tone was low, furious. She looked like she could easily slit his throat.

That suited his mood just fine. "My overactive imagination just took a couple of potshots at us." He hauled her along beside him and shoved her into his car.

"Someone shot at us?" she asked as they pulled away.

"Yeah," he said. His laugh was brief, harsh. "Now who's going to admit they're wrong?"

"You're lying. To scare me."

"Is that so?" Infuriated, he swung the car into a no-parking zone, flipped on the interior light, and twisted to shove his left shoulder in her face. "Does this look like a lie?" Blood soaked his jacket sleeve around a long, jagged rip.

Marissa paled. Her hand reached out to touch his arm. "You're hurt," she said shakily.

Jack had never thought to hear that fragile tone from her. "No kidding. It's just a flesh wound; I'll live. Lucky for me you're a doctor," he added sarcastically. "You can treat it when we get to the hotel. First we're going by a police station, though. I need to report this and let my chief know what happened."

"I'm not going to a hotel. I'm going home."

"You're going where I damn well tell you to go. Tomorrow we'll go back."

"It couldn't have been Jerome. He's in Fort Williams." She sounded off balance, even desperate.

"Probably." He pinned her with a grim gaze. "In case you've forgotten, sweetheart, Jerome isn't the only one who might want you out of the way."

"You think—you think Roth—"

"A phone call isn't tough to make. You're bright enough to figure this out, Marissa. Do you think that little episode was a coincidence? No one's that gullible, least of all you."

They finished the ride in silence.

"Terrific," Corelli said, looking around the dingy hotel room.

Marissa didn't say a word. She hadn't asked where they were staying and she didn't care. There was a chance, growing slimmer with every passing moment, that she could make it to the shower without breaking down. With single-minded determination she pushed past him.

He slapped his hand on the bathroom door before she could shut it in his face.

"Get out of my way," she said.

"Not a chance, baby. We're going to talk. Now."

"The hell we are," she said, and shoved her knee into his groin.

He doubled over, cursing, groaning from pain. Slamming the door shut, she locked it, then turned on the taps and began stripping feverishly. A part of her felt bad that she'd hurt him. She should have seen to his wound, should have been calm, should have dealt with everything in a rational manner. But she couldn't.

The water blasted hot and strong as she turned her face up to it, and she allowed her control to slip. For a moment she was ten years old again, too proud to let anyone know how much her father's latest desertion had hurt her. Here, under the water, she had no need to hide her feelings. Here, in her private world, she could let them out and try to deal with them.

Tears flowed, not easily, but with a slow, tortured rhythm. She hadn't begun to run dry when the door smashed into the wall and Corelli jerked the shower curtain back. Huge, forbidding, menacing, and mad as hell. His anger was tangible, it lay on the air like raindrops.

"Big mistake, Marissa."

It wouldn't be her first one. "Can't you have the decency to leave me alone? Just leave me the hell alone, Corelli! I can't take much more." How had she ended up naked, screaming like a fishwife at a man who upset her equilibrium merely by existing?

"Neither can I." He turned off the water. "Get out."

"Make me," she said automatically. Another mistake, she realized too late.

His eyes glowed even brighter. Fury burned in the brown-black depths, as well as another kind of passion. *What did you expect, you idiot? You're standing here stark naked and Jack Corelli is obviously no eunuch.*

The next thing she knew, she was hanging upside down over his shoulder while he strode from the bathroom. Impervious to her wild attempts to injure him, he moved forward relentlessly and dumped her on the bed. Landing on her back, she tried to catch her breath, bracing herself for what was coming. What she expected didn't happen. Instead, he threw his leather coat over her, covering her from the waist down.

"Wrap that around you before this conversation takes a major detour." His heated gaze traveled the length of her body before stopping at her face.

Stunned, she stared at him. She wondered what would happen if she did nothing. She was afraid to find out. Alongside her anger, a wild sexual furor rocketed through her bloodstream. Her hands shook as she slipped his coat on, wincing when she felt the stiffness in the ruined sleeve.

"Don't press your luck," he told her, his voice harsh and gritty. "I can still cuff you to the bed."

Marissa was no fool. She knew it would take very little to push him over that edge of violence he balanced on. But she was on an emotional edge herself. Pressure had been building since the day Juju Jerome had taken her hostage. Then Gil had called, the ember to spark the explosion.

"Tell me why you left," Corelli said.

She looked down, buttoning his coat, as if it would

somehow hold her together. "You know why, that's how you found me. I needed to see my ex-husband."

"Why did you think you had to come alone?"

"This is my private life. It's not a paragraph of police business."

His mouth a hard line, his eyes narrowed, he stared at her. "Are you getting back together with him?"

She choked back a harsh bark of laughter. "Hardly. He's dying."

Softly, he asked the next question. "If he weren't dying?"

Now she did laugh. Tears rolled down her cheeks as the laughter grew more unbalanced. Even as she lost control, a compartment of her mind analyzed what was happening. Hysteria—full-fledged hysteria. In another person, Marissa would have forgiven it. In herself, she couldn't. She expected more from herself and hysteria was a mark of weakness. Weakness she couldn't afford.

The bed gave with his weight. He gathered her in his arms and pulled her onto his lap. "Don't. Shh, baby, don't cry. God, I hate to see a woman cry."

"I'm not crying," she choked out, clutching him around the neck and burying her face against his chest. He was so big, so strong, so . . . comforting. Everything about him was powerful, potent, masculine.

"Shh, it's okay." He stroked her damp hair. "He's a fool."

"No, he's gay." His hand stilled, then began to stroke again. She thought she heard a muffled curse. Once started, her tears wouldn't stop. The problem with always maintaining control, she knew from past experience, lay in what happened when you finally lost it.

"You're still in love with him." Not a question, a statement.

The tears stopped abruptly. "No." Suddenly it was important that he believe her. Staring at him, she said it again. "No." His skeptical expression told her what she thought. She pulled his head down to hers and kissed him.

She tasted just like he remembered. Hot, sweet, sexy as sin. He wanted to stop kissing her nearly as much as he wanted to continue. But he didn't stop. He stroked his tongue inside her mouth and slid his hand underneath the leather coat to caress bare, warm skin. His mind screamed *mistake*, but his aching body couldn't have cared less.

"I'm breaking all my rules," he said, knowing it was too late to stop. Had it been too late from the beginning? He stroked her breast, heard her sharp intake of breath, felt the nipple tighten against his palm. She felt better than his dreams, and his dreams had been damned imaginative. "You've just blown them all to smithereens."

"What rules?" Her hands worked at the buttons of his shirt. She darted her tongue into his mouth, a light, teasing, arousing touch.

"Don't get involved with a witness." One of the coat buttons came undone. "Never, ever get involved with a smart woman." Another button surrendered. Her breasts peeked out invitingly. "Keep my mind in control and my pants zipped." His mind clouded as he spread the coat open, slid it down over her shoulders and arms, and laid her back on the bed. Naked.

Her body invited him to play out every fantasy he'd ever had about her. Her voice turned sultry, expanding on the invitation. "You haven't broken the last rule. Yet," she whispered, and placed her hands at the snap of his jeans. "What will it take to convince you to break it?"

"Damned little," he said, and covered her mouth with his. He cupped her breasts and caressed her nipples while she struggled with the snap. It gave way and he felt her go to work on the zipper. When she slipped her hand inside his briefs, he stopped her.

"Uh-uh. If I'm going to break my rules, I'm damn sure going to savor the process." He held her wrists manacled above her head with one hand and bent to draw her nipple into his mouth, sucking strongly. Closing her eyes, she moaned and arched her back, her hands jerking against the restraint.

His hand glided down to play with the curls between her thighs. Her hips rose, silently asking for more. Happy to indulge her, he slid a finger deep inside her, unable to stop a groan that echoed hers. Dimly, Jack was aware that making love to Marissa was a monumental mistake. It's just sex, he told himself. But if that were all it was, then why couldn't he remember the last woman he'd been to bed with? Why was he ignoring all his rules—and all the risks?

She pulled her hands out of his grasp. After shucking his jeans, he turned back to her just as she reached for him and tried to peel his shirt off. Jack jumped and swore as the fabric, stuck fast with dried blood, resisted. How could a desire be so strong, it made him forget he'd been shot?

"Oh, God, I'm sorry." She leaned over him, her expression a mixture of guilt, concern, and passion. "I forgot you were hurt. Let me take care of it."

Pulling her head down, he captured her mouth. "Later," he murmured against her lips. "The bleeding's stopped, just leave the shirt. Right now there's another part of me that needs taking care of worse than a lousy flesh wound." He placed her hand on his erection. "I've got a problem here. Think you can help me out?"

She smiled wickedly, mischief dancing in her eyes. "Relax. I'll take care of everything." Stroking her hand up and down his length, she added, "Trust me. I'm a doctor, remember?"

Somehow, in his fantasies about her, he'd missed the one about *her* making love to *him.* Reality just might kill him.

Kneeling over him, beautifully naked, she spread his shirt open and kissed his neck, then strung kisses across his chest until she reached his nipples. A flick of her hot, wet tongue made him shudder and grab for her. He thrust a finger inside her again, then withdrew it and thrust once more. Slow, making love to her with his hand.

"Overestimated," he managed to say.

"What?" Her tongue tasted him, and her hands moved gently, skillfully over his erection.

"I'll have to savor next time." If the magic she performed on him was any indication, her skill as a surgeon wasn't overrated.

She pulled down his briefs and gazed at him. He heard her breath draw in. A moment later she met his eyes, her own harboring a horrified expression, as if something terrible had just occurred to her. If Jack hadn't suspected what the problem was, he might have been concerned.

"Second thoughts?" he asked her with a provocative smile.

"No, but . . ." She shuddered as he moved his hand, slipping another finger inside her. "Do you—" She moaned, arching involuntarily at the movement of his hand. "Do you have a condom?" she asked in a strangled voice.

Jack hooked a hand around the back of her neck, bringing her close enough that her breasts touched his chest and their lips were an inch apart. "I was never a Boy Scout, but I always liked their motto. Look in my wallet." He withdrew his hand, wringing another gasp from her as he did so.

"Thank God," he thought he heard her say.

Moments later she lowered herself onto his aching flesh and he anchored her with his hands on her breasts. Not a sign of ice in her now, he thought. She was pure explosive energy as she took him with her on a hard, fast race to paradise. Rolling with her until he was on top, he drove inside her with a near violence she welcomed with the answering lift of her hips, with her nails digging into the skin of his back. Again and again, he withdrew and plunged in, feeling the pressure build until her muscles contracted spasmodically, and she cried out with her climax. Seconds later, with a final deep, uncontrollable thrust, he followed her.

Jack had rolled off Marissa, but his uninjured arm held her cradled against his side while his hand lazily caressed her hip. Just as she'd suspected, he'd been rough, exciting, and full of surprises. Like surgery, which might help to explain her fascination with him. The tenderness that ran beside the roughness surprised her the most.

An unfamiliar desire to demonstrate a little tenderness herself sneaked under her normal reserve. She jumped out of bed instantly.

"Where are you going?" he asked her sleepily.

"To find my purse," she said, covering her momentary lapse with professional concern. "I think I've got a suture kit in there."

His gaze followed her as she prowled the room. "Can't you just steri-strip it? I don't like stitches. And I can think of other procedures I'd like a lot better."

"I'll bet," she said, smiling. "Nobody likes stitches. But we'll see. Come to the bathroom where I can see the wound better."

He grumbled, but he did it. Luckily, she almost never cleaned out her purse and the suture kit was indeed in there. She soaked his shirt where the blood had dried and carefully peeled it off. Relieved, she saw he'd been right when he said it was a scratch. The coat had protected him. Besides, even Jack Corelli couldn't have done what they'd just done if he'd been too badly injured. At least, she didn't *think* he could.

Though it didn't seem to bother Jack to roam around naked, Marissa wore her camisole and panties. Even so, Jack made it hard for her to concentrate on the task at hand. "If you don't stop that, I *am* going to put in stitches," she told him when his good hand slipped inside the camisole. He withdrew his hand, but before long she felt it sliding along her hip. Finally, she put a bandage over the wound and sighed with relief.

"You're an incredibly difficult patient," she told him.

He rose and gave her a wolfish grin. "Want to reform me?"

"You should rest," she said as he pulled her with him into the bedroom.

"Right. With you wearing nothing but this"—he stopped to push a strap off her shoulder—"silky thing?"

He pushed her gently onto the bed, but she placed a hand on his chest before he could become too distracting. "Why three condoms?" she asked him. It bothered her, more than she liked. As though having one was acceptable, but more wasn't?

"Because," he said, sliding the camisole up until it rested above her breasts, "sometimes they break." His tongue trailed a liquid fire between her breasts.

"That explains two," she said, endeavoring to remember the point. "Not three."

He raised his head and smiled at her. "I told you, I like to be prepared. But I know where you're headed with this, so I'll just cut it short. You're the first woman I've taken to bed in over a year."

"But—"

"And no, the condoms aren't that old." His mouth covered hers and she succumbed, for the moment, to the pleasure.

Feeling the need to reestablish control, she said, "This is just sex."

"Great sex," he murmured in agreement, his hands busy.

"It won't last."

"Right."

"We're totally unsuited to each other."

"Mmm-hm." Now he was nuzzling her belly button.

She pinched him hard, right on the left pectoral, satisfied when he jumped and stared at her in surprise.

"Why'd you do that?"

"You're not supposed to agree with me, you clod. At least, not so cheerfully."

His grin was disgustingly appealing. "Marissa, can we postpone this discussion for another time? Right now"—his tongue traced her navel and slipped lower—"there are more important things requiring my attention."

Her hips rose as his mouth found its goal. "If you insist," she managed to say.

Tonight she wanted oblivion. No past, no future. She wanted a night in the arms of a man who could drive every thought but pleasure from her mind. And Jack Corelli was that man.

SIX

If Jack had needed anything more to convince him that making love with Marissa had been a whopper of a mistake, his reaction the next day proved it beyond doubt. He couldn't stop thinking about her. About making love with her the night before. About doing it again—and again. He spent the drive back from Houston and what was left of the day mooning like a lovesick puppy and fighting a losing battle to concentrate on his job.

Not that anything much was happening there. Jack doubted the shooter had been Jerome. He was probably still holed up someplace in Fort Williams. No, Jerome hadn't followed her to Houston. The Phoenix, though—all the Phoenix had to do was make a call. Plenty of folks wanting work.

That didn't explain, though, how they had known that Marissa had left her apartment or where she'd gone. The possibility of a leak from within his department couldn't be ignored, though there were other police task forces involved. As well as the FBI. Investigating the leak wouldn't be easy.

Since his injury, Jack's partner had been out of the loop on the Phoenix case, and after his release he'd spent most of his time guarding Marissa. So Jack turned to Sergeant Natterhorn for help. There weren't a lot of people Jack felt he could trust in a touchy situation like this, but Gabe was one of them.

As soon as Jack had called from Houston, Gabe had begun the investigation. He'd found nothing yet, neither in their own division nor in the Organized Crime Task Force sharing the case with them.

As Jack was leaving the station that evening Gabe stopped him. "Forgot to tell you, Lieutenant. Captain King was looking for you yesterday. Did he ever catch up to you?"

"Yesterday? No, when was it?"

"Seems like I saw him in your office when you were talking to the chief about going after Dr. Fairfax."

"He wasn't there when I got back. Are you sure you don't have the time mixed up? Maybe he came by after I'd already left."

Gabe shrugged. "Could be. See you tomorrow."

Odd that King would come by again so soon after the last time, Jack thought. He'd call him tomorrow and find out what was up.

Man, I've got to be crazy, Jack thought, standing outside Marissa's apartment. He was actually going to walk in that door and tell her no more sex. No man in his right mind would do that.

But he had no choice. He'd allowed himself to get

much closer to Marissa than he should have. It had to stop, now, before it really began. All of his previous reasoning still held true. He couldn't afford to get involved with his witness. Couldn't afford that vulnerability.

Unfortunately, he was already involved. And if Marissa had been hard to resist before, she'd be damned near impossible to resist now. The fantasy had tempted him, the reality blew him away. He was in trouble, big time.

Locking up after Hank left, Jack tugged on his collar and tried to think of a good way to explain things to her. Failing that, he opted for the direct approach.

"Marissa, we need to talk."

"All right," she answered. Unlike most women, she didn't say anything more. She simply waited for him to speak while idly stroking her cat with those skillful hands.

Because he was afraid he'd chicken out, he said it more brutally than he'd intended. "Last night was a mistake. It should never have happened."

Her face showed only polite interest. She crossed her legs and leaned back into the couch, contemplating him. Beside her, Rosalyn watched him with a nearly identical blue-eyed scrutiny.

"The shooting or the sex?" she asked after a moment.

He stared at her openmouthed, then a reluctant smile crossed his face. "Both. But I was talking about the sex. We can't—I can't afford to get involved with you. It can't happen again."

"You don't want to have sex with me again." She might have used the same tone to discuss the weather.

Was she kidding? Of course he did. "Uh—that's not exactly what I—I mean—" Aware he was making a mess of things, he floundered, sinking deeper into the morass. "Oh, hell!" Throwing his hands up, he finally said, "It wouldn't be a good idea." He felt himself flush and cursed silently.

Marissa's expression hadn't changed a bit. Dr. Ice, in the flesh. Completely indifferent, she stared at him for a long, unblinking moment. "Okay." She rose from the couch.

Stunned by her total lack of reaction, he asked, "*Okay?* That's all you have to say?"

"I wasn't aware there was anything else *to* say."

"You're mad as hell, aren't you?" She must be, she had to have some sort of reaction.

"Should I be?"

His eyebrows lowered as his ire rose. "I just walked in and told you last night was a one-night stand. You mean to tell me you're not mad?"

"Jack." She shook her head, smiling ruefully. "We're both adults. We can admit that last night would never have happened if it hadn't been for a certain set of . . . circumstances."

A muscle jumped in his jaw. Arms crossed over his chest, he leaned a hip against the dining-room table and gazed at her grimly. "Circumstances," he repeated.

"Yes. Danger, excitement. I was upset about—well, I was upset. You were upset. One thing led to another and . . ." She spread her hands. "We ended up in bed together. It could have happened to anybody, given the situation. After all, you were angry, I was naked—"

"I remember," he snapped. God, as if he could ever forget. "Anybody. Meaning you went to bed with me because I was the closest available male. No, make that the closest available *straight* male."

Carelessly, she lifted a shoulder. "More or less."

"Bull."

An emotion he couldn't name flickered over her face. Guilt, pity, he wasn't sure which, but he was damned sure he didn't like it.

Crossing the room to him, she laid a hand on his arm. "Now I've hurt your feelings. I'm sorry, I didn't mean to imply last night wasn't—" She paused, searching for the word. Her gaze collided with his. "Nice," she finished. "It was quite pleasant." Her fingers trailed along his forearm before dropping free. "Really."

When she reached the hall, she slanted him a devilish look over her shoulder. Her bedroom door didn't slam, it closed quietly behind her.

"You're going to pay for that one, Marissa," he promised.

Crawling. Marissa swore she'd have him crawling before the night was out. No man—neither Jack Corelli nor anyone else—was going to toss her aside like yesterday's garbage. She had spent her childhood being pushed aside, left behind, feeling like she wasn't good enough. She sure as hell didn't intend to let Jack make her feel that way now.

It was her own fault, she realized, for thinking that he would be different. Her own fault for granting him the power to hurt her. His reaction shouldn't have mattered, and the fact that it did infuriated her. She didn't expect—or want—an avowal of eternal devotion. But she hadn't expected to be dumped the next day, either.

If anyone was going to call a halt to things, it would be her.

She had just finished unbuttoning her blouse when her bedroom door slammed back against the wall and two-hundred-plus pounds of bruised ego filled the doorway.

"Nice?" he snarled. "Pleasant?"

His eyes flashed nearly black with anger. His jaw was clenched tight, his voice gravelly. Jack Corelli looked like a man with homicide on his mind.

And that was exactly where she wanted him—on the edge of control. She hadn't imagined he'd let her comments pass. She'd gone for a man's most vulnerable spot—his ego. Bent on revenge, she slid the scalpel in deeper and twisted it.

"Why, yes." Her blouse fluttered to the floor, and her fingers paused at the zipper of her skirt. Keeping her expression mild, she added, "Didn't you think so?"

His hand shot out to grip her wrist. Slowly, inexorably, he pulled her closer until he towered over her, his powerful chest rising above hers. With his free hand he took hold of her chin and tilted her head back, glaring down at her. "You're good, sweetheart, I'll give you that. Smooth as Irish whisky. But I'm not buying the routine."

Despite her best efforts, she knew that fury blazed from her eyes. News flash, Corelli, she thought. You're about to find out you don't call all the shots.

"Did you ever consider," she asked him, "that it's not a routine?"

"Liar," he said softly. "You thought the sex was dynamite."

"Did I?" she asked, just as softly. She rose on her

toes, letting her breath flutter across the hard line of his mouth. "Prove it."

He released her wrist and framed her face in his hands, his thumbs resting at the pulse of her throat. A pulse now fluttering wildly, like the frantic beat of a hummingbird's wings.

"Damn you," he said. "I swore I wasn't going to do this." His lips curved into a killer smile, then he crushed his mouth to hers.

Her head fell back, more in abandon than surrender. He yanked her bra straps down as she grappled with his shirt, impatient for bare skin. His lips burned an imprint on the skin of her shoulder, across her breast, then fastened on her nipple through the fabric of her bra. Shocked at the raw pleasure, she arched into him.

When he raised his head, they stumbled toward the bed, flinging clothes aside as they went. He tumbled her onto her back, sideways across the bed, with his hard thigh shoved between her legs.

She spread her hands over his bare chest, shuddering at the heat he gave off, at the feel of smooth, solid muscle, virile masculine strength. Craving him, she combed her fingers through the hair that ran down the middle of his chest and disappeared into the waistband of his jeans.

She felt a primitive thrill when he ripped her bra open and buried his face between her breasts. His mouth wreaked new havoc as he laved her breasts with attention, sucking on her nipples roughly, stopping just this side of pain. At the same time he rocked his leg against her, the rhythm pushing her farther along the edge of the chasm. The chafing of his beard on the tender skin of her breasts made her arch and groan, begging silently for more. Her arms came up to cling to his neck, but she couldn't keep her hands still, couldn't stop them from running down his back to grip his buttocks and urge him to finish what he'd started.

"Condoms," he said, breathing hard. "Did you—"

"The dresser," she answered, just as breathlessly.

He left her for a moment. When he returned he was naked, beautifully aroused, standing over her, the angles of his face sharpened with passion.

She rose to her knees in the middle of the bed, nude except for a pair of white bikini panties. "I bought them today."

Leaning a knee onto the mattress, he dipped his head to kiss her lips. "I never had a chance, then." He handed her one of the packets and added, "Did I?"

Her hand closed around the package as his arms closed around her, bringing them together from chest to thigh. His mouth heated on hers, his tongue probing hard, insistent, unrelenting. He released her only long enough to help her to fit the protection over his rigid flesh, then their mouths fused together again.

She whimpered once, against his lips. He shoved his hand into her hair and tugged her head back. Their gazes met and held. With an urgent move, he ripped her panties off and threw them aside.

"Now," he said.

"Yes, now," she whispered, sinking back on the bed, strangling on the breath-stealing need consuming her. She kept her eyes open, watching him as he entered her with a fast, solid lunge. He withdrew and thrust back inside her once, then twice. Writhing, her hips rising to meet him, she crested on a wave of sensation and exploded. His mouth covered hers, swallowing her cry. Moments later she heard his moan, felt him shudder, shaking with his own release as she climaxed again before collapsing limply beneath him.

"God, you're incredible," he said, long minutes later. "Who won?"

She bit his lip and laughed. "I don't know," she admitted, soothing the hurt with her tongue. "Should we try for best two out of three?"

"Good thinking. Just give me a minute to recover."

"A minute?" She raised an eyebrow and grinned. Sobering, she gazed at him. "I wanted you to crawl. You didn't."

He carried her hand to his lips and watched her as he kissed her knuckles. Then he turned the hand over to press an intimate kiss into her palm. As solemn as she, he said, "For you, Marissa, I probably would have."

"Dr. Fairfax," Marissa snapped irritably when she answered the phone. The clock showed 1:03 A.M. She never enjoyed being awakened in the middle of the night, but she detested it when she wasn't even on call.

"Sorry to disturb you, Dr. Fairfax," a male voice said, "but could I speak to Lieutenant Corelli?"

Marissa started to hand Jack the phone, but luckily she woke up enough to realize she had to pretend to go farther than her own bed to find him. She wasn't at all sure she was ready to go public with this relationship. Not yet, anyway.

Jack took the phone from her. "Corelli." He listened a second and sat straight up. "Tony's *where?* It's one in the morning. He's never— You're sure it's Tony?" Cursing crudely, he reached across her to slam the receiver down on the hook.

"Get up," he told her. "Come on, Marissa. Get dressed."

She cracked open an eye. "Does insanity run in your family? I'm not going anywhere except back to sleep."

"I've got to go to the station. You're coming with me. It'll take too long to wait for a backup."

"No," she said, burying her head under the pillow. "Go 'way."

"Marissa." The bed creaked when he sat beside her. "Please."

Shocked to hear the word and the tone that went with it, she removed the pillow and stared at him. Corelli didn't plead, he ordered. "What is it? What's so important?"

His back to her, he started pulling on his jeans. "I've got to go get somebody out of jail." He slipped a FWPD sweatshirt over his head. "My son."

He'd never mentioned a son. It made her realize how little she knew about him. "Why is he in jail? What did he do?"

"They popped him for burglary, but I don't believe he did it. There's bound to be a mistake. When I find out who made it . . ." He let the sentence trail off, but the furious set of his face told her the rest.

Marissa rose and began to dress. "Give me three minutes."

"Thanks."

❖———❖

When his father walked into the room, the atmosphere changed. He was a cop, he was in charge. He was his dad. Tony wanted to run to him, to say he was sorry, to swear he'd never do it again. Wanted nothing so much as to ask his father to get him out of this mess and make it all go away. Then he remembered and pain slammed into him anew.

Liar. Both of his parents were liars.

"It's about time you showed up," his mother said.

"Get him out of here," his father told her, jerking a thumb at Welch.

"He's Tony's counsel. Don't you order him around, Jack." His mom's voice was shrill, like it always was when she was upset. Tony figured she was madder at him for getting her out of bed in the middle of the night than for his being caught burglarizing a store.

His dad said something he would've grounded Tony for a month for saying, then he turned to the slime. "Get out, Welch. Tony doesn't need counsel, and if he does I'll get a juvenile defender."

"My client's mother retained me, Corelli. Which she had a perfect right to do, I'll remind you."

"That so?" His dad jabbed a finger into Slimeball's chest. "*I'm* your client's father and *I* say your ass is fired. Now get the hell out of here."

"You'll be sorry for this, Corelli. The kid needs all the help he can get," Slimeball said, and left.

His mom and dad started yelling at each other. "What is *she* doing here?" Elena asked, pointing at the woman who sat in a chair in the far corner of the room.

"Don't worry about Marissa, she knows how to keep a confidence. Tony's your concern, not her."

His father's new girlfriend, Tony thought. It had to

be. Across the room, their gazes met. His stomach churned. His dad had brought his girlfriend to the jail with him. Tony knew his father. That could only mean he was serious about her.

"This is private," his mother screamed. "What in the hell do you mean dragging your—"

"Elena. Drop it." His voice, a honed knife, sliced through the rest of her sentence.

Tony looked away from the blonde, back to his parents. He didn't blame his mother for shutting up. When his dad used that tone, even his mother paid attention.

Jack turned to Tony. "The arresting officer said you admitted to being the lookout at the site of the robbery."

Tony didn't want to stay in this place. It smelled, it smelled like fear and other worse, nameless smells, and he already hated it. But he wasn't going to talk to *him*. Why bother? He'd just lie some more. Tony crossed his arms over his chest and slouched back in his chair.

"So?" he said, shrugging insolently. "What about it?"

Jack didn't blow up, as Tony half expected, but he stared at him for a long time. "What's going on, son? You've never hung with this crowd before."

Son.

Liar! Don't call me that! Tony wanted to scream the words, but he was afraid to. He wanted to put his head down and cry like a baby, but he couldn't do that either. He didn't answer.

His dad continued. "This time you'll get probation, but you might not be so lucky next time."

"Big deal." He looked at the floor, at the wall, at the

blonde again, as rudely as he dared. Everywhere but at his dad.

"You'll be released to your mother's custody tonight. I'll be over tomorrow and we'll discuss your punishment."

That brought his head up. "You just said I'd get probation."

"From the judge. The juvenile system might only slap your hand, but I won't." Jack leaned close to him and said softly and carefully, "Your butt's in a sling with me, son, and you're going to have to work like the devil to get out of it. You think about that when you get home. Think about what it would have been like if you'd had to stay here."

"Who cares?" Tony muttered, fighting back tears.

"I do. And your mother does. I don't know what's going on with you, but you can be damn sure I'm going to find out." His hand fell on Tony's shoulder and squeezed, offering comfort along with the harsh words. But Tony couldn't accept the comfort and pulled his shoulder away.

His father and mother moved to a corner of the room, and even though he couldn't hear them, he knew they were arguing. So what else was new? They argued all the time. Hoping to keep from crying, Tony looked at the blonde again. It didn't help much. For once, Slimeball was right. She was hot. Smokin'. His fists clenched helplessly. His dad would marry her, just like his mom had said. Then he'd forget Tony like he was used gum. Unutterably weary, he leaned his head against the wall and closed his eyes in despair.

❧━━━━━━━❧

Marissa had rarely been as conscious of wanting to be someplace else as she had at the jail, sitting in on Jack's discussion with his son and ex-wife. She didn't belong there. He knew it, she knew it. Why had he taken her, why had he made everyone even more uncomfortable? It certainly wasn't because he wanted her opinion. On the way home he hadn't spoken a single word.

He finished checking the apartment and strode back into the living room. Grim-faced, unapproachable, the cop was in charge with a vengeance.

"Why did you make me stay there?" she asked. "Why wouldn't you let me wait for you in your office?"

He shot her a brief, hard look. "Just because I'm sleeping with you doesn't mean I trust you."

Her stomach rolled, heaving with a sudden pain. The unexpected attack hurt, and so did his low opinion of her. "I thought you understood my reasons for leaving. You can't think I'd take advantage of you while you were trying to help your son." But he did think it, she could see that.

"Look, Marissa, I do what I have to do." His shoulder lifted and fell. "You can't be trusted, so I took you with me. You're going to be protected whether you like it or not."

Her own temper flared in answer. "This anger is directed at yourself. And Tony. Don't take it out on me, I don't need it, Corelli."

"Well, well, Dr. Fairfax. When did you find time for a psych residency?" Leaning a shoulder against the wall, he gave her a nasty smile. "Are you a shrink now, as well as a surgeon?"

"No, but it doesn't take a psychiatrist to figure out

your problem here. If you need to talk, I'll listen and try to help. Otherwise, I'm going to sleep. I have to go to work in a few hours." She left him standing in the living room and shut the bedroom door behind her.

A little while later she felt the mattress give as he crawled into bed with her. Gathering her in his arms, he pulled her spoon fashion against him. At first she held herself rigid, but after a minute she relaxed. Though she was still angry with him, she knew he was hurting—and she wanted to help, she wanted to heal.

"I'm sorry." His breath stirred her hair. "You didn't deserve that."

"No, I didn't. What was that about, Jack?"

He lay quietly for so long, she thought he wouldn't answer. Nothing broke the silence until a low roll of thunder sounded. Rain splattered against the windowpanes. The wind rose and the storm howled its despair, a low, plaintive wail of distant thunder.

"It rained the night I found her," he said.

SEVEN

"Rain." Jack's voice was soft, husky. Not angry, but infinitely sad. "Rained like a son-of-a-bitch, so dark, dark as midnight sin. Thunder, lightning, wind howling like a hound from hell. When she was little, my sister, Natalie, hated the rain. She used to come get me and make me read to her before she'd go back to sleep. She said the words kept her safe. But she was never safe.

"Natalie was crazy about this kid, this punk who was our neighborhood gang leader. I'd tangled with him before." His shoulders shook with what might have been a laugh. "Man, I tangled with everybody back then. In and out of juvenile hall, in and out of jail. In trouble, but mostly solo trouble. No gangs for me. I had enough trouble boiling inside me that I couldn't put up with somebody telling me what to do. And then I got lucky. When I was sixteen Burt King busted me and decided I was worth saving."

Marissa didn't interrupt. She let him talk, offering the comfort of a warm body, the understanding of silence.

"King harassed the hell out of me. Found me a job, pushed me to go back to school; he even tried to find someplace to help my mother, but she was beyond help by then. All she wanted was the bottle, and to be left alone. So I left her alone. Burt tried to help Nat, too, only she wouldn't take any help. I did, because I had ambition. I knew I didn't want to end up like the junkies, the dealers, the winos. Or like my old man. The sorry SOB ran off when I was five and never came back."

Jack released her and sat up in bed, resting his back against the headboard, hooking his arm around his knee. An occasional flash of lightning illuminated his harsh profile—the strong lines of his cheekbone, nose, and mouth—and the shock of straight, dark hair falling over his forehead. She remained silent, but she kept her gaze on his face, waiting for the rest of the story.

"Nat wouldn't listen to me, she thought I was lame to take up with a cop. More than she wanted anything else, she wanted to belong somewhere. People like us don't belong, though. She bounced from foster home to foster home. Every time she came running back to the neighborhood, to the gang. To the gang leader. For six months she was happy because he let her be his girlfriend. When he got tired of her he sold her to a pimp. Her first john beat her to death. I found her in the alley behind our apartment." He turned his head and looked at her, no expression on his face. "She was fourteen."

Marissa put her arms around him and held him. At first she didn't speak, she simply held him, waiting for the sharpness of his pain to ebb. "I'm so sorry," she said at last. "You must have loved her very much."

"She was all I had," he said simply. "Our

mother—she was dead long before she actually died. Natalie was the only family I had."

"You tried to help her. It was her choice, Jack, not yours."

"She was a child. My responsibility."

"No, not yours. Natalie was your mother's responsibility, and she failed her. You were a child too. What else could you have done? You can't make other people's choices for them. Not those kind of choices, anyway." Gently, she stroked his back. If he had a bullet wound, a tumor, a disease, she could help him. Wounds of the soul were beyond her abilities to heal.

He pulled away from her. "Tony knows Natalie's story. He *knows*. I told him so he'd—so he'd understand. Because I knew I couldn't stand to fail again. Not with my son." Anguished, confused, he locked his gaze with hers. "Why would he do it? Why? When he knows what could happen?"

Her heart twisted, hearing his pain. "I don't know. Maybe a counselor—"

Vehemently, he shook his head. "Counselors didn't help Nat. Or me."

And he hated them for it, Marissa thought. "That doesn't mean counseling won't help Tony. If he's changed so drastically, there's bound to be a reason for it, Jack. Take him to someone who might convince him to talk."

"I don't know. Maybe . . . God, I don't know."

For the short time before dawn he slept in her arms. The rain had eased to a patter, but the thunder still throbbed in the distance.

And sometime during that night she fell in love with him.

❖────────❖

Trouble raining down was one thing, Jack thought, but this was a friggin' typhoon. He stared through the windows of the OR door and watched Marissa work. The woman was a magnet for trouble. Pray God she didn't get another deathbed confession. His nerves wouldn't stand it.

When he'd arrived at work that morning, four days after Tony's disaster, he'd heard Roth's case had been moved up and would go to trial the following week. That was the good news. Then Gabe had rained on him with the bad.

"Roth is in the hospital," Gabe had said, his bloodhound face looking even more mournful than usual.

"He's where? What happened?"

"Somebody found the safe house. The two guards, one of our men and an FBI man, are dead. Roth was critically wounded. Worse, we don't have a clue who it was."

"Whose night—" Jack broke off, suddenly remembering who had pulled guard duty last night. "Oh, God, it was Broadhurst, wasn't it? Dammit!" It wouldn't have been any better if it had been another one of his men, but Broadhurst—he was so damn young. Only weeks before, Jack had gone to his baby's christening. One more widow, one more fatherless child.

Forced to shove aside his sorrow and regret, Jack put in a call to the FBI agent assigned to the case. "See what you can find out from homicide," he told Gabe while he waited for the agent to pick up.

"Right. Want me to get to the scene?"

"Yeah. Don't let the feds give you any grief, either.

This is as much their screwup as ours. Hell," he said, hanging up the phone and rising. "I'll talk to him later. Which hospital?"

"FWC," Gabe said.

He was halfway out the door when he heard Gabe yell after him, "Dr. Fairfax has the case."

So here he was, waiting for her outside the OR, trying unsuccessfully to figure a way to keep her under protection if Roth died. A corpse couldn't go to trial. Therefore, Marissa would no longer be a material witness. Therefore, she would no longer need protection.

Except from Juju Jerome.

Thirty minutes later Marissa came out of surgery, stripping her cap and shoving her hand through her hair. For an instant she rested her fingers on the bridge of her nose. Blood spotted her surgical gown, and her face was so pale, she looked like she could keel over any minute. Lines of exhaustion were etched around her eyes, which didn't surprise Jack. He wondered how she kept going at the pace she worked, knowing she'd been awake and operating for most of the past thirty-six hours.

Squaring her shoulders, she faced him. "He's going to SICU—surgical intensive care. I don't know whether you'll be able to question him or not. You'll be informed if and when you can see him."

"Dammit! Is he going to die?" With Roth dead as well as Lemont, they had absolutely nothing.

"There's a high likelihood that he'll never pull out of the coma. I'm sorry. He could go anytime now."

"Not your fault," he told her. Humpty-Dumpty was cracking six ways to hell and Jack couldn't do a thing about it. Unless they found out who shot Roth. Maybe the feds already knew, but Jack had a feeling they didn't.

He sent Hank home with Marissa. She was still under protection—unless Roth died. And she was so beat, she was out on her feet. Jack didn't want her going home alone.

Half an hour later Roth died without ever regaining consciousness. Jack would have to tell Marissa she was no longer under police protection. He smiled without humor. At least one of them would be happy.

Jack didn't get to Marissa's place until after midnight. Preliminary investigations into Roth's death had turned up a big fat goose egg. The FBI were as clueless as everyone else about how the killer had found the safe house. Still nothing definite on Welch, either. A miserable, rotten day, all in all.

He let himself in, leaning down to scratch the cat's head as she greeted him. Rosalyn rubbed against him, then tried to jump up onto the dining table, but she missed by a mile. A little surprised, Jack picked her up and carried her with him into the bedroom.

When he crawled into bed, Marissa turned over and flung her arm across his chest, snuggling against him. Sometimes he wondered whether a class act like Marissa could ever be happy with somebody like him, but since he was nearly certain they wouldn't last, he didn't dwell on it for long.

"Any leads?" she asked him sleepily.

"Zippo."

She rose on one elbow and looked at him. "Want to talk about it?"

He smoothed a hand over her tousled hair, trailing the ends through his fingers. "Go back to sleep, you're beat."

"I've been asleep all day. Talk to me."

She didn't push, she offered, with the understanding that he could take it or leave it. Maybe that was why he started talking. Wrapping an arm around her, he settled her against his side and rested his chin on the top of her head.

"Tony's attitude still sucks. His counselor's seen him three times in the last four days. According to her, he's surly, obnoxious, uncommunicative, and crying out for help. And he won't talk to her." Jack didn't really blame him. He didn't much like the counselor, either.

"Give him time, Jack. Give her time."

His hand stroked her arm absently. "Don't have much choice. The kid sure as hell won't talk to me. I've tried and all I get is the same crap he hands the therapist. Elena—he wasn't talking much to her before this happened. Now she says he hardly speaks." He brooded on it, wishing he knew the answer, but just now he wasn't even sure of the question.

"There's more, isn't there? Tell me the rest."

She'd taken his hand, and he thought how odd it was that she could communicate comfort through such a simple gesture. "Yeah. My case against the Phoenix ring is going down the toilet. Roth died."

"I was afraid he would. You never got to talk to him, did you?"

"Nope. That's not all, though. With Roth dead, that means you're off the hook, Doc."

"Off the hook?"

He watched the import of what he'd told her sink in.

"You mean—"

"Dead men don't go to trial. Officially, you are no longer in need of police protection." He turned her face up to his and pinned her with a serious gaze. "But before you go singing the 'Hallelujah' chorus, remember that doesn't mean you're out of danger. There's still Jerome."

Puzzled, she asked, "Why would he kill me now? The trial won't take place, he has no reason to."

Sighing, Jack shook his head. "You've got to understand how these people think. You know he skimmed from the organization. You're unfinished business and he's a punk with nowhere to go but a fast ride to hell. Jerome won't stop until you're dead, or he is."

"Did you ever consider that you might be wrong?"

"No." Jack turned over, drawing her underneath him, and looked down into her eyes. "I'm staying with you at night. Don't ask me not to."

"Jack—" Her eyes scanned his face. "I won't. I want you to stay."

"Good, because I'm going to. If I could keep you in custody, I would. Dammit, I hate this, but there's nothing I can do." They stared at each other silently. "Promise me something." Lowering his head, he kissed her neck, nuzzling at the hollow. "Promise me you'll be very, very careful, until I find Jerome."

"I will," she whispered. "Make love with me."

"I will," he answered.

The minute she opened the apartment door he blasted her. "Where the hell have you been? Not two days ago you told me you'd be careful. So what do you do? You disappear for three hours without even a note. The damned cat isn't even here. I thought you'd taken her and skipped town." Why did she do these things to him? She made him crazy. Now she had him ranting like a madman.

"I'm sorry. I forgot."

Her voice held all the liveliness of a broken windup toy. Jack took a closer look, noticing her pallor and the emptiness in her eyes. With a Herculean effort, he softened his voice. "Where did you go?" She had better have a damned good excuse.

"The vet's." She hung her purse on a chair. "Remember when I told you that Rosalyn had been acting strangely? I thought maybe she had a touch of something."

He stared at her, unable to believe his hearing. "You let me make myself crazy so you could take your cat to the vet? Couldn't you have called?"

"I told you, I forgot."

Still no expression in her voice. "Where's the cat?" he asked. The back of his neck tingled. Jack didn't like the vibes he was picking up. "Where's Rosalyn? Why didn't you bring her back?"

"Rosalyn has—" She hesitated, then continued, "Rosalyn had cancer. Inoperable. Dr. Morgenstern put her to sleep."

"Oh, God, Marissa." He put a hand on her arm and squeezed. "I'm sorry." Jack knew how much she loved that cat. He'd watched her play with her a hundred times. Seen her groom her, feed her. Marissa used to sit on the couch and stroke her for hours. The cat was the first thing she looked for when she walked through the door, the last thing she looked at as she left.

Feeling like a heel, he tried to apologize. "If I'd known, I wouldn't have yelled at you."

"No, you're right." She stripped off her coat and threw it over a chair before she went into the kitchen. "I should have called."

He followed her. "You were upset. It's okay, baby, I understand."

Her eyes looked almost normal when she glanced at him. Almost. "Do you want me to fix something to eat, or have you already eaten?"

He stared at her. My cat's dead, are you hungry? Talk about repressing your feelings. "Marissa." He touched her arm again, wanting to comfort. "It's not a crime to be upset. Most people would be."

Her gaze was cold and empty when it met his. "I'm not most people."

"You're not a machine, either."

Her lips thinned. "The sympathy is appreciated, but I'm fine. I'm sorry she's dead, but I'll get over it."

"Just like that?" He stared at her again, unable to grasp her reaction. It didn't jibe, didn't add up.

"Jack," she said on a note of impatience, "I deal with people dying almost daily. Do you really think I'd get hysterical over a cat?"

Not hysterical, but he expected some show of feeling. Maybe it did jibe, though. Her walls were up, and she wouldn't let anyone breach them. Least of all him. "You can't let anyone know you're real, can you? That you've got real blood running through your veins instead of ice water. You're afraid to feel too much, so you just pretend you don't feel anything."

"Maybe you're wrong. Maybe I don't feel anything."

Was he wrong? Could she really put her cat to sleep and feel nothing, beyond a flicker of sadness? He didn't believe it. "Don't hide your feelings. I'm the only one here, no one else has to know."

She slapped a palm down on the drainboard. "You don't get it, do you? There's nothing to hide."

"You're afraid to let me near, aren't you? Afraid to break down in front of me, just like you can't let loose at work. You're afraid to let me close." And he'd thought Marissa had no fears.

"This is ridiculous. We're sleeping together. That's not close enough for you?"

He took a step toward her. "No, it's not. That's a different kind of closeness, one you can handle. Sex touches your body. But this . . ." He touched his fingers to her temple. "This would touch your mind, your emotions, and you're scared spitless to let me do that."

"Be careful what you ask for, Corelli," she warned him. "You might not like what you get."

"For God's sake, Marissa, all I'm doing is offering you a little comfort and you can't deal with it."

"No, you're imbuing me with emotions I don't have. And you're angry because I don't. Get used to it, Jack, because you're seeing the real me."

"That's a load of bull. I know you better than that."

"No, you don't." Her voice snapped out flat and final. "If I need your help, I'd ask. I asked you in Houston, didn't I?"

But she hadn't known him then. Not like she did

now. "Yeah, and my guess is you've been regretting it
ever since."

"You're making me regret it now."

She pushed past him. A few minutes later he heard
the shower start. Damn her and that shower. Why
wouldn't she take what he offered her? He wanted to
help her, comfort her, protect her.

Who was he kidding? He loved her. What a stupid
thing to do. Fall in love with a woman who couldn't,
wouldn't, even share the pain of her cat's death with
him. What would she do if he told her he loved her?

Right the first time, he thought. She'd run like hell.

Marissa turned her face up to the water, but gained
no solace from it. She couldn't cry, couldn't let loose,
not this time. She couldn't afford to lose control with
Jack. Not now that she knew him, now that she loved
him.

He was so damned decent. His decency had surprised her at first, because he hid it. Unless someone
needed him. It made her angry that he gave so much,
that he never seemed to count the cost to himself. If
someone needed something, he gave it, no questions
asked. Didn't he understand that you couldn't afford to
give so much of yourself? Didn't he understand that
feeling too much was dangerous?

Oh, the man was diabolically good at edging past
her defenses. Look at what had happened when she
cracked in Houston and let him comfort her. No more
weakness, she had to be strong. She couldn't afford to
count on him; she couldn't count on anyone besides

herself. Not even the man she loved. Especially not the man she loved.

"Lieutenant?"

"Yeah." Bleary-eyed, Jack looked at Gabe, standing in his office doorway. With Marissa on duty the night before, he'd taken advantage of her absence to work all night. Not that it had done him much good. He was still zero for zero. Nothing on Roth's killer, nothing on Jerome's whereabouts.

Gabe walked into the office, shutting the door behind him.

"Tell me," Jack said, before Gabe could speak, "why Jerome is so damned hard to find. The little weasel just vanished into thin air. Or into the city's belly, anyway. How did he do it?"

Gabe spread his hands. "Maybe because he looks like every other two-bit hustler out on the streets. Nothing to distinguish him from a hundred others." Shifting uneasily, he stuffed his hands into his pockets and cleared his throat.

His odd manner gave Jack the first clue that something was up. "So, what can I do for you?"

"It's kind of . . . personal, Lieutenant."

"Girlfriends giving you trouble again, Gabe?"

"No, sir. I meant personal for you."

Puzzled, Jack frowned at him. "Lay it out for me."

Gabe again shifted from foot to foot, looking even more uncomfortable. "Did you ever find out what Chief King wanted the day he came by your office? You know, the day you followed Dr. Fairfax to Houston?"

"No, to tell you the truth, I'd forgotten all about

it." The night Gabe had told him about it, he'd had other things on his mind. Marissa, mainly. "Why? Does it matter?"

Gabe didn't answer, he merely looked at him.

"You can't think Burt King has anything to do with this." Burt, involved with Phoenix? Jack shook his head. "No way."

"He was in your office. Had access to all sorts of things. Nobody would think a thing about it. Everyone knows you two are friends."

"You're not even sure *when* he was here. Do you realize who you're accusing?"

"Lieutenant, I'm not accusing him. All I'm saying is you should check it out. Cops have turned bad before."

"Not Burt King." But Jack was already considering Gabe's point. Because he was right, and Jack knew it. If it had been anyone else, he wouldn't have had a problem, but Burt . . . Burt King was the closest thing to a father Jack had ever known. "All right. Dammit, I don't like it, but all right."

"Sorry, Lieutenant. It's probably nothing."

Gabe eyed him as if he expected to get blasted. Jack had to smile. "Don't look so worried. I don't usually ream my men out for doing their jobs."

Gabe grinned. "That's a relief. For a minute there, I thought I'd be lucky to get away with a black eye."

After Gabe left, Jack picked up the phone.

"It's Jack," he said when Burt answered. "Sorry it took me so long to get back to you, but I'd forgotten you were looking for me until one of my men reminded me. Things have been crazy lately."

"Good to talk to you, Jack, but your man's mixed up. I haven't been looking for you."

"It's been a while, maybe you've forgotten. Almost two weeks ago. Thursday before last."

Burt hesitated. "It's possible, but I don't remember. Lord, Corelli, I've slept since then."

He sounded irritated, not altogether out of character for Burt. "Gabe gave me a message and I'd forgotten about it. Guess it wasn't important . . . ?" Jack let his last sentence hang as a question.

"Must not have been," the older man said, and went on to talk of other things.

Obviously, Burt considered the subject closed. Too bad Jack couldn't. Burt King wasn't a forgetful man. If he had been in Jack's office, he'd have remembered it. And Gabe had definitely seen him at the station the day Marissa left for Houston. Much as he hated to, Jack resolved to dig deeper.

EIGHT

Marissa hit the button for garage level six and sagged wearily against the back wall of the hospital elevator. Just as the doors closed a man jumped inside and shoved something into the center of her chest. She looked down to see the barrel of a gun lodged between her breasts. Her gaze lifted to Juju Jerome's face.

He wore pale green scrubs, a white lab coat, a surgical cap, and an expression of satanic glee. "Gotcha," he said, his smile glinting maliciously.

After twenty-four hours of duty, nineteen of them spent on her feet, Marissa was almost too tired to comprehend what was happening. Almost. Fear roiled in the pit of her belly as Jerome began to stroke the gun lovingly across and around each of her breasts.

"Let's go for a ride, pretty lady. In that little black car you like so much." He slid the gun underneath her scrub top and T-shirt, trailing it over bare skin.

Cold. So cold. Death would be cold, she thought, like the gun.

"I've been watching you," he said, his voice chilling,

hypnotic. "Watching you and waiting to get you alone. No cops, pretty lady, just you and me." With the gun barrel he inched her clothes upward, baring her skin to his gaze.

She forced words out, praying he wouldn't realize how terrified she was. "Why?" she asked him. "Roth is dead."

"Phoenix isn't." The elevator doors slid open. His hand closed tightly around her upper arm, forcing her to walk with him toward her car. "Neither is Corelli." He smacked his lips and smiled at her. "Revenge tastes sweet. You'll taste even better."

Fear choked her. So he wouldn't kill her quickly. He meant to drag it out, make her suffer, make her plead for her life. Too soon, they reached her car. Jerome told her to open the passenger door, then shoved her in, forcing her to crawl over the gearshift to the driver's side.

"Start the car," he ordered. "We're goin' on a magic-carpet ride." He laughed, filling the car with evil.

Maybe the malevolent, self-satisfied laugh did it. Or the feel of icy metallic death gliding lasciviously over her body. It might have been the knowledge that she had nothing to lose. Whatever triggered it, something broke the spell of fatal lassitude, the fog invading her mind.

Not by a flicker of her eyes did she betray the welcome change, the flooding resurgence of her wits and will to live. She placed her hand on the stick shift. Power, the perfect weapon, in the palm of her hand.

Jerome lowered the gun and smiled again when she

cranked the engine. "That's it, blondie. Ready for a good time?"

Surprise, Jerome. She jammed the car into reverse, backed out of her space, shot down the ramp, and accelerated into the turn before he could even begin to react. Jerome yelled, screamed, but she ignored him, concentrating on her driving. Thank God, the garage was nearly empty. Innocent bystanders would slow her down and she meant to give Juju Jerome the ride of his destructive life.

"I'll shoot you, bitch!" Wildly, he swung the gun back to her. "Slow down!"

Braking on the straight, she allowed the rear end to swing wide and connect with a rail. "Shoot me and you die, Jerome." Her voice was calm, even, in direct contrast to his blustering rage.

Again she stomped on the gas, pushing as fast as she dared to and still remain in control. She didn't watch the speedometer or even shift gears. The Porsche would do over fifty in first. If she drove that fast in a parking garage, they'd be splattered from one end to the other in seconds.

Marissa remembered her father's words. "Feel the car, live the car. Every tremor, every vibration, every shudder of speed should live in your bloodstream as you drive. Become a part of the car. You *are* the car." She had never imagined the day she would use the only legacy her father had left her to save her own life.

Jerome still screamed, but he'd pulled the gun away from her. Thank God for small favors. She managed to ignore the sickening scrape as the side of the car kissed the wall in a long, electric slide. Jerome alternately cursed, moaned, and shouted. The wilder, the more out of control the ride, the more frightened he'd be. And she wanted him terrified, as petrified as she'd been only minutes before.

She thought she'd gone too far the next moment. Seconds into the turn the car slid into an uncontrolled spin, the rear bumper slamming into a concrete post before rebounding off it into the straight again. The stench of burning rubber rose, surrounding her like an elixir of hope as she fought the wheel and mastered the car once more. Jerome's terror, dead quiet and tangible, shuddered in the air as they cleared the last level, crashed through the barrier, and shot out into the street.

At last, Jerome found his voice. "You're crazy! Freakin' nuts! Stop!" Terror made his voice shrill.

Marissa smiled and turned the wheel to head straight toward the embankment on their right. With a last hysterical curse, Jerome shoved open his door and bailed out in the middle of the turn. Damn! If only he'd waited a few seconds, she'd have been up to speed. Automatically, she braked, yanked the wheel, and started the skid. She slid sideways, then slammed her foot on the gas. The car headed dead straight at Juju Jerome.

With barely seconds to spare, he managed to scramble out of the way. Maybe she wouldn't have hit him, but she sure as hell wanted him to think she would. But even as her mind registered the fact that he was gone, she didn't stop. She couldn't run the risk that he would come back; she had to get away.

Her arms, her legs, her entire body shook with reaction. Marissa knew it, knew she was out of control now, but she couldn't stop. Neither the trembling, nor the car. Not yet, she told herself, not yet. Don't you dare break down yet. Home. If she could get home, she'd be safe. She would deal with everything at home.

Jack found her car parked in the apartment parking lot. The feeling that something was wrong, terribly wrong, with Marissa had come over him slowly but persistently, about an hour after he'd talked to Burt King. Accustomed to playing his hunches, he hadn't questioned it. When she hadn't answered the phone at home, he'd called the hospital, only to hear that she'd left over an hour before. Instantly, all his alarms had started shrieking. Now, fifteen minutes later and seeing her car, he could have sworn his heart stopped beating.

Her meticulously maintained black Porsche, the car he'd seen her polish until it shone with a reflection as clear as any mirror, looked like the loser in a drunken brawl. The right front fender was smashed, the front bumper dented badly, both rear fenders and the lights destroyed. The entire rear end was a mangled mess. A white scrape, about six inches wide, ran along the entire length of one side.

In less than a minute, he took in the damage to the car, then vaulted up the concrete stairs with his heart literally in his throat. As he burst through her door the sound of the shower had him alternately cussing her for scaring him and thanking God that she was alive.

"Marissa?" No answer. He waited a minute and pushed open the bathroom door, repeating her name, louder. "Marissa!"

Jack pulled back the shower curtain. She was huddled in a corner of the tub, face buried in her drawn-up knees, arms around them, hugging them. The edge of the shower spray beat on her legs and feet.

"What happened? Your car looks—" He broke off when he realized she wasn't responding and reached to turn off the ice-cold water. How long had she been in there? His hand under her chin, he lifted it so he could see her face. She stared at him, through him, her expression absolutely blank.

"Oh, God." Knowing shock when he saw it, he wasted no more time. Wrapping a towel around her, he hauled her out of the tub and carried her to the bedroom. Still unresponsive, she lay curled on the bed staring vacantly while he rifled through her clothes in search of something warm. Finally he jerked a white terry cloth robe from her closet and managed to get her into it.

"What happened?" he asked her again, but gently this time. His brief inspection before he'd covered her had revealed no physical injuries. That made her emotional state all the more frightening. The terry cloth brushed his cheek as he gathered her onto his lap and ran his hands over her, soothing her. "Marissa, tell me what happened." She still hadn't voluntarily moved a muscle or made a sound. Not a whimper, not a sigh, not a sob. Nothing.

"Talk to me, baby. Come on, tell me what happened. I'm here now, you're okay. You're okay." She wasn't, though. She needed heat, nourishment, sugar. Hell, he wasn't sure what she needed. She'd scared him so badly, he'd forgotten what he was supposed to do. Maybe he could get her to drink something hot and sweet. But when he tried to put her down to go to the kitchen, she made her first movement, clutching her arms around his neck.

So he sat and held her, talking to her, soothing murmurs, nonsense sounds, anything to let her know that he was there. He felt her shudder. Her arms tightened and she shuddered again, a long, sustained shaking.

"Jerome."

If he hadn't been holding his breath waiting, he might not have heard her, so softly did she speak. "What did he do? Tell me, Marissa. Talk to me, baby."

"Don't leave me," she whispered. "I was . . . so scared. I'm still scared."

Jack had never believed that a person's heart could turn over, but it happened to his when he heard her words and felt her terror. "Don't worry, I'm right here. I won't leave you." *Ever*, he wanted to add, but he didn't.

Marissa started talking. Slow, halting, in a tone he'd never heard her use, one that didn't even sound like her voice.

"He came into the elevator. With a gun."

Jack didn't ask for details or clarification. Once she told the story, he could go over it with her later for details. Right now the important thing was to let her get it out.

"He kept touching me . . . with the gun . . . touching me, everywhere . . . I knew he'd kill me." She shuddered again. "And he said, before he killed me he'd—before I died he wanted to—he meant to—"

"Don't." Unable to stand more, he interrupted. "Don't think about that. Just—just tell me what happened."

"We got to my car. He thought I'd drive him some-where. He thought he'd make me drive to my own murder."

Her head buried between his neck and shoulder, she'd been speaking against his chest. Now she leaned back and looked at him. The faint, upward curve of her lips eased the tightness in his chest. The old Marissa was still in there. "What did you do to him?"

"Scared him. Before he jumped out, I think he wet his pants."

Jumped out? He wondered how fast she'd been go-ing, but didn't ask. "What happened to him?"

"I'm not sure. I tried—I think I tried to run him over. Maybe, I don't know. He ran away, I guess. And I just—came home."

He didn't ask why she hadn't called him. She'd been in shock by then, a perfectly understandable reaction to what had happened. But he wished she'd called him.

"Frankie," she said. "I keep seeing Frankie, lying there with his brains—"

The thought of Marissa dead was more than he could handle. "For God's sake, Marissa, don't. Don't think about it. It's over, you're safe." Because he was going to find the bastard if he had to put every cop in the city on the streets looking for him.

"They splattered on me, you know. Not like blood does in an operation. More like—" She broke off and shrugged, her tone almost conversational.

Afraid she was slipping into shock again, he shook her. "Stop it," he ordered. "You aren't dead and you're not going to be. We're going to find Jerome."

"Rosalyn's dead."

His mind didn't make the connection, and for a moment he only stared at her.

"When I came back I looked for her. But she wasn't here." She started to cry then. "I'd forgotten she was gone. Forgotten she died."

Jack held her, tried to comfort her, let her cry. His heart ached for her. He'd never felt more helpless in his life, except the night he'd held his dead sister in his arms. At least Marissa was alive, and he was going to make damned sure she stayed that way.

Gradually her tears lessened and stopped. She lay quietly against his chest. Thinking she'd fallen asleep, he started to ease her down on the bed.

"Don't go." Her arms tightened around him again.

He patted her back. "I need to call the department. Get them started on this. I won't take any longer than I have to."

"Sorry. I'm being . . . silly." She drew in a deep, shaky breath. "I'm fine."

"You're a mess." he told her, setting her beside him before rising, "but you're entitled. It'll take a minute." Her face turned up to his, she gave him a tremulous smile. He leaned down and kissed her, for the first time since he'd found her huddled zombielike in the shower. He kept the kiss tender and brief, afraid if he didn't he'd end up making love to her. Right now he needed to be a cop, not her lover. The sooner he talked to headquarters, the better.

At least he intended to be brief, but her mouth softened and clung to his, her breath drew in with a catchy little sigh, and he wanted nothing so much as to lose himself in her and prove to himself she was alive. But he had already failed her by not finding Jerome, by not protecting her when he knew she was in danger, so he lifted his mouth from hers and resolutely laid her back on the bed.

"I'll be in the living room," he told her, and left quickly.

Marissa couldn't go to sleep, but she stayed in bed and listened to snatches of Jack's side of the phone conversation. It consisted primarily of a lot of swearing laced with explosive orders.

"Dammit, I don't give a flying—" she heard him say, and smiled before her thoughts turned to the man who waited to kill her.

Surely the police would find Jerome this time. They had to. She couldn't spend every day looking over her shoulder in fear of her life. If he caught her again she would die, she had no illusions about that. Restlessly, she turned over and listened to Jack. Some of his words reached her more clearly than others.

". . . safe house," he said. "Of course, now. Yeah. Call me back."

Several minutes later he walked into the bedroom, carrying a mug of something. Hot chocolate, from the smell of it. The gesture made her smile. Jack Corelli's cure for everything, from insomnia to attempted murder. The smile left her face.

He set it on the bedside table. "Thought this might help. Do you want anything else?"

"You're putting me in a safe house."

His jaw hardened. "That's right. Don't bother arguing. You're going and that's final."

"I don't want to."

"Marissa, I can't . . . I can't go through this again. I have to know you're safe." He sat beside her on the bed, putting the mug into her hands. "Don't fight me about the safe house." His hand smoothed her hair. "We don't have a choice anymore."

"No, I know you're right. But I don't have to like it."

She hated it. How in the hell was she supposed to spend *days* in the safe house when she was climbing the walls after one miserable afternoon?

Marissa prowled the small apartment in search of anything to keep her mind off Juju Jerome. Nothing worked—not TV, not reading, and after a long nap she couldn't sleep anymore, either. Finally she resorted to forcing the two guards to play poker with her. That helped a little, but unfortunately neither one presented much of a challenge to someone who'd grown up with the game. Aside from racing, poker was the only other useful thing her father had taught her.

"Fleecing my men, Doc?" Jack asked upon his arrival.

"She wouldn't play for money, Lieutenant," Barber, the heavy loser, told him.

"Lucky for you." Jack motioned toward Marissa's winnings, a huge stack of toothpicks. "If you'd asked, I could have told you she has a better poker face than either of you ever will."

"You've never played poker with me," Marissa objected. "How would you know?" Her heart had no business leaping about in this crazy way, just because he was there. What was the matter with her?

"I know your face, Doc," he said. "Seven A.M.," he told the men after seeing them to the door.

"Hank will be here in a minute," he added as he returned to her. He put out a hand and turned her face up. "You look about a million percent better than you did this morning. How do you feel?"

She managed a decent smile. "Pretty good, actually. Especially since I got some sleep. As long as I don't think about—" She stopped in mid-sentence, unwilling to say the name.

"Then don't think about it," he told her.

Taking her hand, he pulled her to her feet and into his arms. His mouth found hers. Pleasure rapidly superseded surprise. Eagerly, she met his kiss and felt life surging through her. The fuzzy unreality that had dragged at her all day receded. She felt warm, alive, loved. Loved? The thought had her tearing her mouth from his.

"Wait, Jack." Because he felt responsible for her, because he desired her, didn't mean he loved her. She felt his lips press against her neck. His hand covered her breast and kneaded it gently.

"I've waited all day," he said, his rough tone at odds with the tender play of his hands.

"Hank," she croaked out. "You said he'd be here any minute."

He kissed her again, deeply, hungrily, igniting desires she wanted him to fulfill, a thirst she needed him to slake. Finally, he withdrew his mouth from hers and said softly, his breath against her lips, "Consider that a promise I intend to keep. Tonight."

He released her and she sat, unable to stand on legs

that suddenly felt like Jell-O. "You can't. Hank's going to be here."

For a minute he looked confused, then his brow cleared. "Don't worry about Hank."

"He doesn't even know we're"—she hesitated, unable to classify their relationship, and finished—"involved, does he?"

Jack shrugged. "I don't know whether he does or not, but I'll talk to him. He knows me pretty well. I don't think he'll be surprised."

Marissa arched a brow. "Oh? Have these flings often, do you?"

"This isn't a fling." He traced his fingers along her cheek, her jawline. "We're way beyond that."

The doorbell rang. "Corelli, it's me," Hank called out.

Their gazes held for a long moment, his fingers still trailing along her skin.

Hank pounded on the door. "Corelli, open up."

His hand lingered for an instant longer, then dropped. As he answered the door Marissa let out an unsteady breath and beat a cowardly retreat to the bedroom.

Leaning back against the closed door, she waited for her composure to return, but it was a long time coming. No, their relationship wasn't a fling, to either of them. But if it wasn't a fling . . . then what was it?

Her drive for independence, her vow not to depend on others, vanished when she was with Jack. She couldn't keep cracking and letting him pick up the pieces. *Face facts, Marissa, you've been on shaky ground from the time Jack Corelli barged full speed into your life.* More like lethally shifting grounds since she'd gone to bed with him. Bad enough that she'd fallen in love with him. Why did a part of her insist that they might be able to work it out?

Jack came into the room a few minutes later, shutting the door behind him. "I talked to Hank. He's clear about us now."

"That's nice," she said. "I wish I was."

Why was he staring at her so oddly? So intently? Why was her stomach a jumble of nerves and her heartbeat revving at the speed of sound?

"I told him we're getting married," Jack said. "As soon as this mess is taken care of."

NINE

Married? He'd told his partner they were getting married? Marissa felt the blood drain from her face as she stared at him. "Are you crazy?"

"Not last time I looked."

"Why would you tell Hank we were getting married? It serves no purpose, and besides that, it's a lie."

"Marissa." He took hold of her shoulders and bent to kiss her lips, briefly. "It doesn't have to be a lie."

Dizzy, she reached for something to hold on to. Jack was the closest thing and her hand closed around his arm. "You can't be serious," she whispered.

Humor lurked in his gaze. "Afraid so," he said, patting her hand and smiling wryly. "I'm in love with you, Marissa. I want you to marry me."

Speechless, she walked to the bed and sat on its edge, staring at him. "This is— You were frightened this morning. You're feeling guilty because you didn't protect me. Don't imagine that means you're in love with me."

He stuck his hands in his pockets and smiled at her

again. A tender smile, one that should have looked odd on such a tough face, but it didn't. She hadn't known he could smile like that.

"How can such a smart woman be so blind? Yes, I was afraid. Yes, I feel guilty. But that's not what this is about. Long before this morning I knew I loved you. I didn't tell you because I knew you'd run if I did. But—Marissa, when I found you this morning, when you told me what happened and I realized how close I came to losing you, I couldn't wait any longer."

"That should have made you run the other way. This is your protector complex talking, Jack. Not love."

Regarding her thoughtfully, he started undoing his shirt buttons. "Haven't you thought about it? About us being permanent?"

Not seriously, she thought, looking away from him. She hadn't dared to, for more than one reason. "No. My first marriage soured me on the idea." Her gaze shifted back to his. "You of all people should understand that. You've never remarried."

A shrug and his shirt dropped to the floor. He sank down beside her on the bed. "Not because I thought the whole institution was doomed. Only because I never found a woman I wanted to marry. Until you." He slid his arm around her waist and slowly trailed his lips down her throat.

"There's more between us than just the sex," he murmured, slipping a hand inside her blouse.

Finding it hard to concentrate, she asked, "Is that why you're seducing me?" His fingers teased her nipple. Her breath quickened automatically.

His grin shouldn't have been as charming as it was, especially since he knew it and used it far too effectively. "Figured it couldn't hurt." In ten seconds flat, he'd removed her shirt and bra. His eyes darkened as he looked at her, darkened even more when he reached out to cup and caress her breasts. Lying back on the bed, he pulled her on top of him. One hand slipped over her denim-covered rear. "Admit it, Marissa, you like it."

Increasingly bewitched, but still struggling, she gave in enough to kiss him. "Sex isn't the only thing to consider." But at the moment she was fighting a losing battle with her body on that issue.

"It's way up on my list," he said, attempting to shove her jeans down over her hips. "Let me make love to you, Marissa." His voice alone could have seduced her, husky with desire, rough with emotion. "I need you now, and you need me."

She did need him. The morning had almost subsided to a hazy dream, but the terror still lurked. Jack could drive those lingering demons away. She moved aside long enough to shimmy out of the jeans, leaving herself clad only in tiny emerald-green panties. Staring at her, he groaned, then started to remove his own pants.

"No, don't." Her hands covered his, and she stretched his arms above his head, straddling him once again. Admitting she needed him was a big step, but she wouldn't relinquish all control. Sighing, she felt his potent arousal throb against her. Though she wasn't sure why, she knew a heady thrill of power that she was nearly naked and he was almost fully dressed.

"You're overbearing," she told him, and rotated her hips, pleased to hear his breath draw in. Leaning down, she kissed him, nipping his mouth with tempting bites, her bare breasts rubbing against his chest. "Autocratic, domineering—"

"Marissa." His voice sounded choked, his hands kneaded her hips mercilessly. "I'm about to explode here."

"And controlling," she finished with another slow revolution of her lower body against his.

"You're on top," he pointed out through gritted teeth. "Driving me crazy. Seems to me like you're in charge."

Taking pity on him, and herself, she helped him get rid of his jeans and briefs and her panties. With her poised on top of him, the hard length of his flesh pressing at her soft warm entrance, he took her face in his hands and looked into her eyes.

"I love you, Marissa. I don't want to lose you."

Her heart ached to hear his tenderness. His eyes were dark, earnest, and she could see the love in them. She wanted him to know the truth, felt compelled to tell him, even if it was a mistake. She kissed him. "I love you, Jack."

Then she took him inside her, and though their lovemaking was rough, with a touch of desperation, it was tender as well. And so beautiful she wanted to cry with joy. She loved him, she knew he loved her—but she was more afraid than ever that she would lose everything. And if she did lose everything, one more time, could she put herself back together again?

It wasn't until much later that night that Jack realized Marissa had never actually agreed to marry him. She lay in the soft light thrown by the bedside lamp, her head on his shoulder, tracing patterns across his chest. It felt good, in fact, she was starting to turn him on again when her fingers trailed farther down his chest, but he wanted to make sure everything was clear.

"Your place or mine?" he asked her.

Her hand stilled. "What?"

"Do you want to live at your place or mine? I guess I should show you my place first, though, before I can expect you to make a decision."

"Jack, wait." She sat up, shoving the hair out of her eyes. "I didn't—I don't—I can't marry you."

Damn, he should have known it was too good to be true. He rose, locking gazes with her. "Did I miss something? Didn't you just tell me you loved me?"

Her steel-blue eyes were as unreadable as ever. "I do love you, Jack. But that doesn't mean I can marry you."

"Why the hell not?"

She got out of bed and reached for her robe, which lay over a chair. With her back to him, she said, "For one thing, there's my job. My hours are worse than yours, and yours are lousy."

He leaned back against the headboard. Jitters, he told himself. She just had the jitters. "So cut back on your hours. I'll cut back on mine. We can work around that."

"It's not that simple, and you know it. You've seen what my job takes out of me. I don't know if I can give you—give us—the attention I'd need to."

"You could do it if you wanted to," he said quietly.

"Jack, what we have is good. Why chance ruining it?"

"Ruining it? Why should marriage ruin anything?

What's got you so scared, Marissa? It's more than your job or mine." Was it her first marriage? Finding out your husband was gay would make anyone gun-shy, he had to admit.

She sat on the edge of the bed, pleating the material of her robe with one hand. That gesture, coming from Marissa, gave him a crystal-clear picture of her inner turmoil. He laid his hand on hers, rubbing his thumb up and down the underside of her wrist. "I know you had a bad marriage. Mine wasn't great, either. But they're not you and me. We can do better than that."

Her gaze lifted to meet his. "I'm not sure I can. I'm not sure I wa—" She broke off abruptly.

"You're not sure you want to," he finished for her. "That's it, isn't it?"

"No, I'm not sure I want to get married. Love doesn't necessarily equal marriage."

"It's a great fling, but forget anything permanent, right?" He couldn't keep the hurt from his voice, or the pain from grabbing hold of his heart. He didn't want a fling with Marissa, he wanted the whole thing with her.

Reaching out, she touched his cheek. Ran her fingers down his jaw. "That's not what I said. I meant it when I said I love you. But I'm not ready to make a decision about marriage."

She hadn't said no, absolutely. It cost him, but he knew that now wasn't the time to press her. If he did, he wouldn't like the answer. He stuck a hand in her belt and pulled her close, kissing her long and hard. "No decisions," he muttered against her lips, praying time would help his cause. "For now."

❦━━━━━━❦

Garbage, Jack thought. He had nothing but garbage on Marissa's case. The wino witness—the only witness—had been having d.t.'s at the time of the attempted abduction. Though the old man had been sitting just outside the parking garage and had apparently seen Jerome make his escape, figuring out what was real and what was a hallucination to the man was hopeless.

Yesterday the damn dogs had lost Jerome's trail at the banks of the Trinity River. The lucky bastard had crawled off somewhere, into the grime and slime of the city's underbelly. But he'd be back. After what Marissa had done to him, that was something Jack knew for dead certain. Jerome would return, and God help them all if he got hold of her again.

And now he had to deal with another mess. Jack looked down at Burt King's file, then lifted his gaze to Gabe's face. "This," he said, waving at the file, "isn't enough to indict him."

"No, but it's enough to launch a full-scale investigation."

"Dammit!" Jack pounded his fist on his desk. "All this started more than two years ago, before he retired. Ever since his wife's death, he's been dirty. I knew it hit him hard, but who'd have thought he'd be suckered by the first gold digger who came along?" Disgusted, he picked up a glossy photo and threw it toward the sergeant.

Gabe tapped a finger on it and whistled. "Yeah, but a drop-dead-gorgeous gold digger."

"You figure he started taking bribes then." Jack figured it, too, but he would rather hear Gabe say it than have to state King's crimes himself. If it were anybody but Burt, he kept thinking. But it wasn't.

"Looks like," Gabe said. "Timing's right. The stings started . . . going wrong more often. Sometimes King called them off, sometimes it seemed like the gang got wind of the sting before it happened."

"King was the leak. And this is just the tip. There's no telling what else he did. God, I can't believe I'm doing this. Investigating Burt King for taking bribes."

Gabe shifted uncomfortably. "Lieutenant, if this all pans out, then King knows who the boss is. The Phoenix. King knows him. Are you going to offer him a deal?"

His gaze met Gabe's. "He's dead for sure if he goes to jail. You know that, I know that, he knows that."

"So you are going to deal with him."

Already weary, though it was only ten A.M., Jack passed a hand over his brow. "I don't know what I'll do, Gabe. But one way or the other," he said, staring grimly at the photo of the woman who'd been the beginning of King's destruction, "Phoenix is going down. That's a promise."

The very last thing he needed, Jack thought when he got to the safe house that night, was for Marissa to get a wild hair to get out of there, but that's what happened. And his partner, seated at the table studiously ignoring the two of them, hadn't done a thing to help him.

"What kind of a harebrained scheme is that?" he asked her after she'd told him her latest idea. "Do you really think I'd let you be the bait in a trap for Juju Jerome? You've lost your mind."

"Not yet," she snapped, flashing those gorgeous baby blues at him, "but I will if I have to stay here any longer. See, just like I said, you're doing it again."

"Doing what? Not agreeing to this insane idea you've dreamed up?" Let Jerome have a chance at her again? When he didn't think he'd ever recover from the last time?

"Taking charge, having to be the one in control," she said, poking her finger in his chest. "Refusing to listen to anyone else. You're not going to find him. Has the decoy policewoman at my apartment lured him out?"

Jack wondered how he could want to strangle Marissa, protect her, and make love to her all at the same time. "No. But we're working on another option."

"Sorry, but you're out of options and I'm out of time. I can't stand this, Jack, I can't."

He put a hand on her shoulder. "Baby, I know it's hard, but we'll get him." They had to. Because he couldn't stand it, either, couldn't go on like this, worrying about her every second of the day.

"It isn't hard, it's impossible. We can't wait forever for Jerome to make a move. You have to let me do this so I can get back to work."

"The hell I do." He wasn't risking her again. Period. No matter if he had to keep her locked up for a month.

"You're not protecting me, you're suffocating me. How can I even consider marrying you if you won't respect my right to make choices?"

"This isn't a matter of respecting your rights, for God's sake, it's a matter of safeguarding your life." He looked to Hank for support. "Explain this to her."

"Sorry, Jack." Hank shrugged. "I agree with Marissa. Jerome isn't moving. Maybe he's hurt. Hell, he could be dead and we wouldn't know it. We can't expect her to sit in this little apartment forever. Something tells me she isn't keen on that idea. Besides, I don't like night duty as a steady diet. My wife likes me to come home at night." He winked at Marissa.

Jack snorted.

"But I think Jerome's alive," Hank continued, "and so do you. And he's not falling for the decoy, Corelli. We're going to have to let Marissa go back to work and lead as normal a life as possible if we want him to surface again."

"No. Dammit, no!" Furiously, he turned to Marissa. "Do you have any idea how dangerous he is now? After what you did to him? You humiliated him, Marissa. Emasculated him. Jerome—he'll be like a rabid dog after the number you did on him."

"Then he's bound to make a mistake. If he's that emotional he won't be thinking clearly," she said, as though her logic were irrefutable. She laid her hand on his arm, forcing him to pay attention. "We have to draw him out. I can't spend the rest of my life like this."

Jack knew he was fighting a losing battle, but he wasn't ready to give up. "Not yet. You'll just have to live with it another day or two. I haven't given up hope that we'll round him up."

❖———❖

Two days later and not a flipping sign of the sucker. Jack stomped into the safe house and slammed the door behind him.

"You win."

Seated at the dining-room table with the ever-present cards, Hank and Marissa simply stared at him.

"I can't find the bastard," Jack said. "I've had every man I could spare and then some looking for him. He's not showing himself. There's nothing left to do but try to flush him out. So you two win. I'm arranging for twenty-four-hour guards on you tomorrow, Marissa." Pray God the guards would be enough.

Frustrated, he dug in his shirt pocket for a cigarette, forgetting he'd thrown his last pack out days ago. Finding none, he cursed under his breath and wondered why he'd ever thought quitting seemed like a good idea.

Marissa watched him with a half smile on her face. "Jack." She rose and came to him, laying a soothing hand on his arm. "You're making the right decision. You'll see."

Hands jammed in his jeans pockets, he didn't touch her. "I've got a bad feeling about this."

Hank spoke from his seat at the table. "Corelli, you're a little too close to this case to be objective. It's the best decision you could make in this situation."

Jack's hard gaze met his partner's. "I hope to hell you're right, because if we've guessed wrong . . ." He let his voice trail off, since everyone there knew the answer. If they guessed wrong, Marissa was dead.

Tony slumped against the wall, waiting for his dad's girlfriend to answer the door. Marissa, he was supposed to call her. He didn't want to call her anything, he didn't want to be there. And he wasn't stupid, no matter what *they* thought. Tony knew what was going down. They were setting him up for a big-time fall.

His dad poked an elbow in his ribs. "Straighten up. You want her to think you're a slob?"

Tony didn't much care what she thought. Digging his hands in his pockets, he mumbled, "Yeah," and slumped even more against the wall.

She opened the door and smiled at them. "Hi, Tony. I'm glad you could come."

Right. Tony didn't say anything, he just shoved past her and went inside. His dad was looking at her like . . . like she was the sun coming out after a long, cold winter. He'd never seen his dad look at anyone that way before. Then he handed her the pizza boxes, and Tony saw that she looked at him the same way. His stomach twisted and turned over.

"Did you get the supreme?" she asked his father.

"Sure. Here, let me help you." Jack followed her into the kitchen while Tony stared around the living room. Not much of an apartment for somebody who was supposed to be loaded. He heard them talking, but he couldn't make out the words. Then he didn't hear anything. Tony knew what that meant.

If he were Jack's *real* son, he wouldn't be worried. If he were his *real* son, he could be sure his dad wouldn't blow him off for another kid. But he wasn't his real son, he wasn't his blood.

"Come on, Tony," Jack said, "let's eat."

She tried to talk to him, telling him to call her Marissa, pretending she wanted to know stuff about him. What did she care? She didn't want him, she wanted his dad. Soon enough, she'd have him and Tony could say *adios*.

"How's soccer going?" Jack asked.

"Fine," Tony mumbled.

"What position do you play?" Marissa asked him.

Tony looked at her, and without answering, stuffed another slice of pizza in his mouth.

"I could have sworn you had some manners once upon a time," his father said grimly. "Answer Marissa's question."

"Forward," he said sulkily, his mouth still full of food. His dad was giving him a look that meant he was in for it. So what? he thought. What else was new?

"Is your team doing well this season?" Marissa asked, not giving up.

"Nah."

After they finally figured out he wasn't talking, they quit asking him questions and talked to each other. It shook him up even more to hear them talk. Marissa and his dad weren't like his mom and Slimeball. They actually seemed to *like* each other. And they talked, really talked to each other.

When they'd all finished eating, Marissa rose and started clearing the table.

Sick of waiting, Tony turned to his father. "Why don't you just get it over with?"

"Get what over with?" Jack asked, looking confused.

"Tell me what you dragged me over here for."

His father's face went grim again. "I 'dragged' you over here to meet Marissa. You got a problem with that, you can tell me why."

"Already met her," Tony mumbled. "Remember?"

"Yeah, well, I wanted you two to talk somewhere besides the city jail."

"You never made this big a deal over a babe before. What's so great about her?" Besides killer legs.

"Lots of things. And Marissa's not just any 'babe.'" Jack smiled at Marissa, one of those smiles that meant he thought she was special.

Tony wanted to throw up. Or cry.

"Why are you being so rude? What are you trying to prove?"

"Nothing." He slumped in his chair. "You must think I'm really dumb. I know you're already shacked up with her. Go ahead and tell me the rest."

Marissa made a choking sound, but she didn't speak. His father had his angry face on now. Tony wondered if he'd hit him if he pushed him far enough. Jack had never hit him before, but there was always a first time. Slimeball said that a kid as mouthy as he was needed slapping. Maybe his dad would start to think like that too.

"I don't think you're dumb," Jack said, "but you're treading on thin ice, Tony. Lose the attitude before you get into even more trouble than you're already in." When Tony said nothing, Jack continued, "We've talked about getting married, if that's what you're wondering."

Duh. Like he didn't know that. "Yeah. I figured." Insolently, he stared at Marissa, but he spoke to his father. "Why do you want to marry her? 'Cause she's hot or 'cause she's rich?"

Total silence. Marissa's face paled and she flinched like he'd hit her. It should have made him feel good, but it left him feeling mean—like slime. Like Slimeball.

"That tears it!" Jack jumped up, knocking his chair over, and jerked Tony to his feet. Tony braced himself for a pop, but it didn't come. He almost wished it would. "Apologize right now. And don't *ever* say anything like that again."

Refusing to speak, Tony stared at him. He hated them, he hated them both for doing this to him. For lying. For not wanting him and pretending like they weren't going to kick his butt out of their lives.

"Apologize," Jack repeated, his voice quiet but commanding.

His gaze fell before his father's glare. "Sorry," he finally mumbled, afraid to push any further. "I didn't mean nothin'."

Marissa cleared her throat and looked uncomfortable. His dad called somebody—backup, he said. A little while later a cop came to the door and Jack took Tony home. The lecture on the way home didn't much matter. He felt like he couldn't sink any lower, anyway.

Tony waited until he got to bed to cry. He'd show them, he'd show all of them.

"Don't say it," Jack said when he returned from his ex-wife's house.

Ruefully, Marissa shook her head. "You have to admit, it's another problem. And one we hadn't really considered." As if they didn't have more than enough to start with, she thought. Their jobs were difficult enough, and that didn't even begin to address how she felt about having to depend on a man again. Besides, she wasn't at all sure that Jack could ever allow her the independence she desperately needed. His nature was so protective, she didn't believe he could change it.

"God knows, I don't blame you for not wanting to marry me after that little demonstration, but—"

"Don't be stupid, Jack," she interrupted. "You know it's got nothing to do with Tony's rudeness. The problems were already there."

"What does it have to do with, then?" He sat beside her on the couch, propped his elbows on his knees, and looked at her. "Are you ever going to tell me what the real problem is?"

She could see that he was holding his temper in check by the way the muscle in his jaw ticked. "I told you—"

"No, you gave me some line about our jobs. And we both know that's an excuse."

Her own temper flaring, she shot back, "It's not an excuse. My work is important to me and I can't just toss it aside because you want to get married." That was true, though it wasn't the whole answer. But she couldn't give him all the reasons now. Even if she couldn't agree to marry him, she wasn't ready to lose him.

Jack flung a hand up in frustration. "No one's asking you to forget your work. Don't you think I know what it means to you? There's something else, something you're not talking about."

"I'm just not as sure as you are that marriage is the best thing for us."

For a minute he looked at her, his eyes bleak. "Maybe you're right," he said wearily. "You sure as hell say it often enough."

Perversely, she found she didn't like him to agree

with her. Deep down, she wanted to believe that marriage was possible. But every time she thought about depending on a man again, depending on him to love her, she wanted to run. Feeling guilty, she attempted to make it up to him, at least in some small measure.

"Tony doesn't hate me, he feels threatened by me. We should have expected it. Given the circumstances, it's a natural reaction. He'll come around once he realizes you're not going to forget him just because you might remarry."

"Will he?" Jack shook his head. "I don't guess it matters, does it? It looks to me like he doesn't have anything to worry about."

Still wanting to comfort, Marissa said, "Jack, I don't want to fight with you. Let's go to bed." He looked so tired, so dejected, she thought, watching him rub a hand over his face.

"Might as well," he said. "We're sure as hell not going to get anything accomplished when you won't even talk to me."

She wished she could talk. That she could explain it to him. Would he understand that she was terrified to depend on a man? Men let you down. They *always* let you down. It was as simple as that. Loving Jack was hard enough. Marrying him would be impossible.

Several hours later Marissa struggled out of a sound sleep to answer the phone.

"Marissa, I've got to speak to the lieutenant."

Even half-asleep, Marissa thought Gabe Natterhorn didn't sound like himself. From what she'd noticed,

Gabe never seemed to hurry, but his voice revealed an ominous urgency. She handed the phone to Jack.

"Corelli," he said, groggily. "No. Oh, God, no." The anguish in his voice brought her fully awake. "He isn't—" He listened a moment and said, "Thank God for that. Thanks, Gabe. I'm on my way."

"What?" she asked him, sitting up as he sprang out of bed and began jerking on his clothes.

"Tony's on his way to the hospital. He was involved in a gang fight—knives, not guns. Gabe didn't know how badly hurt he was, but he was alive when the paramedics took him."

TEN

"He's alive," Jack repeated as he pulled on a sweatshirt, hope mixing with despair in his voice.

Grabbing for the scrubs she kept easily accessible, hanging on a hook on the closet door, Marissa tried to give him what little comfort she could. "It may not be serious. You know they take any kind of trauma to the ER, especially a child. Is that all the information you have?"

"Gabe was heading a sting operation on a gang. One of Phoenix's gangs, we suspected. Tony—" He hesitated, then looked at her. "What the hell was he doing there?"

She shook her head, wishing she had an answer for him. Since she didn't, she concentrated on what she *could* do. "What's his ETA?" Thank God she lived only five minutes away from the hospital.

He glanced at his watch. "Eight to ten minutes now. Can we beat him there?"

"It'll be close, but we can try," she said, tying her scrub pants. "Do you want me to drive?"

Jack tossed her his keys. "Too bad your car's still in the shop."

He said nothing more until they had almost reached the hospital. When he spoke, his voice sounded intense, edgy. "Will you take care of him?"

Jack's son. She thought about him as she'd seen him earlier that night. Young, belligerent—and deep down, scared spitless. Of what? Oh, Lord, what if . . . what if he died? Could she handle that? No, but she didn't think she could deal with it any better if she didn't take his case. If she refused and the worst happened, she would always wonder if she could have saved him. Double jeopardy.

"I'm not exactly uninvolved in this. I'm not sure how objective I can be."

"I don't give a damn if you're objective or not," he grated out. "I've seen you work, Marissa. You're the one I want. You're the one I trust."

She glanced over at him, then turned her attention back to the road. "People—doctors—can make mistakes if they're too involved with the patient." And the patient's father, she thought, but she didn't add it. God, she ached for him. "Jack, any of the doctors up there will do their best. I'm not the only competent one. Yerber is an excel—"

Savagely, he interrupted. "Will you do it, or won't you? It's a simple question. Just answer it."

No choice. Her hands tightened on the steering wheel. She had no choice. "Yes."

"Good." He relaxed a fraction after that, but Marissa only grew more tense. They reached the hospital just after Tony's ambulance arrived.

She and Jack hit the entrance doors together. The

din and the smells of the ER assaulted her senses. Impressions struck and filtered through her brain in seconds, a crazy kaleidoscope of sound and sight. Friday night. Full moon. Madhouse.

In impassioned Spanish, a woman implored one of the nurses to let her take her husband home. A man sat on the edge of a gurney, rolling his head on his shoulders and chanting softly. Shrill cries from a child were interspersed with a woman screaming that she didn't want to have the baby after all and please make it stop.

The smell of blood mingled with the aromas of Betadine, Lysol, and other antiseptic odors. The staff had ordered pizza, and whiffs of pepperoni juxtaposed nauseatingly with an occasional stench of vomit. Friday night at FWC ER. A typical night, except that it wasn't. Not for Marissa.

As she passed the desk she fired a question at admissions. "The knife wound that just came in, which treatment room and who's got him?"

"Yerber, in two," the admissions clerk said, glancing up. "But Dr. Fairfax," she protested to Marissa's back, "you're not on call tonight."

Marissa didn't bother to answer. Outside the treatment-room doors she turned to look at Jack and laid a hand on his arm. "I'm going to let you come in with me. You can see him, and if he's conscious, you can let him know you're here, but then you'll have to leave. Promise me you'll leave without me having to order you thrown out. Don't push me on this. I swear I'll do it if I need to."

His tortured gaze held hers for a heartbeat of time. "All right," he said. "Whatever you say, as long as I get to see him first." He followed her into the room.

He looked so damned young lying there on the gurney with his eyes closed. Jack reached out and touched Tony's hand, as much to reassure himself that he was still alive as to let him know he was there.

"Shocky," he heard Yerber say. "Intermittently conscious."

Tony's eyes opened. Hazel eyes, flecked with pain and confusion. Jack remembered seeing the same panicked expression two years earlier, when Tony had broken his leg at soccer practice. Jack smoothed his son's sandy-colored hair back from his forehead. "You're at the hospital, Tony. They're going to take care of you."

"Hurts. Hurts bad." His eyes drifted shut.

"Possible pneumothorax," Marissa was saying, her face smooth, expressionless. "Let's get a chest X ray." She looked at him across Tony's body. "It would be better if you left now, Jack."

"Are you telling me to leave or asking me?"

She hesitated a moment. "Move out of the way and you can stay."

Immediately, they wheeled a machine—the X-ray machine, he guessed—over to the gurney. The scene took on a surreal quality, as if stepping away from the table gave him an illusive distance. He wasn't distanced, though, not this time. His son lay on the table fighting for his life. Jack wasn't a cop now, he was simply Tony's father, and scared down to his soul that his son would die.

Rubbing his hand across his forehead, he tried to concentrate on the orders Marissa snapped out, the responses of the other doctors and the nurses. A jumble of impressions assaulted him, a sense of the frenetic pace that trauma demanded. Tubes and blood and instruments flashing. Marissa, calm and controlled, her healing hands moving rapidly over Tony's body.

"Blood pressure's eighty over sixty and still falling," a woman's voice said.

Marissa held the X ray up to the light and studied it briefly. "Rule out pneumothorax. Penetrating wound to the abdomen, shock, deep wound to the left flank under the ribs indicate a possible splenic or liver laceration. We've got to get that bleeding under control. Okay, I want him in the OR, ASAP. Move it." Her tone was quick, sharp, decisive.

The team started to wheel Tony out of the room. Marissa came to stand in front of Jack. Her gloved hands were bloody. Tony's blood. Jack fastened his gaze on her eyes, trying to read them. Dr. Ice, he thought fleetingly. Every inch the surgeon, those steel-blue eyes hiding every thought.

She spoke gently but rapidly. "He's going to the OR. All the signs—acute abdomen, shocky, the position of the wound—indicate internal bleeding. I want to operate as soon as possible. You or his mother need to sign the permission forms for surgery."

Surgery. That sank in, but not much else did. He asked the question uppermost in his mind. The only question that really mattered. "Will he live?"

Marissa stripped off the gloves. "Jack, I won't know how serious it is until I get in. There are too many wild cards to be able to predict exactly what he'll require. With the high likelihood of internal bleeding, I don't have time to wait around to find out."

Calm, cool, professional. Wasn't that what he'd

wanted for Tony? Then why did it anger him at the same time? "Don't give me any double talk. What kind of crap is that? Can't you just tell me what's going on?"

Her gaze didn't falter. "No. Not until I get him on the operating table. I'm sorry, but that's the way medicine is."

"You'll know when you know," he said grimly.

"That's about it." She put her hand on his arm and squeezed. "I can't give you a definitive answer. Not yet."

When he followed her out of the room, he saw Elena standing beside the gurney, clutching Tony's hand and asking questions hysterically. He wondered how he was supposed to deal with Elena when he was barely maintaining control himself.

The instant she laid eyes on Marissa, Elena shrieked, "What are you doing to my son? Where are you taking him? What's wrong with him?"

Marissa's voice, in contrast, was soothing. It held the same tone Jack used when he needed to calm people down. "Tony is shocky. I think he has internal bleeding. I suspect it may be a laceration of the spleen, possibly the liver. Whichever it is, we need to stop that bleeding."

"Surgery? And *you're* going to do it? Who—" She stared at Marissa, shaking her head before turning to Jack. "I want another doctor to take care of him. I don't want her operating on my son."

"Jack asked me to take Tony's case," Marissa said, still with that same unperturbed, professional demeanor. "If you have a problem with that, Dr. Yerber would be glad to take over. He's an excellent surgeon."

"No," Jack said. "I'll handle Elena. Go on and do

what you have to do." He closed his hand around Elena's arm and dragged her aside.

He took a deep breath, willing himself to be calm, knowing he couldn't afford to lose it now. "You are not screwing around with Tony's life, Elena. Let Marissa do the surgery."

Her eyes were wide, wild with emotion. Fear, Jack realized. God, of course she was afraid. Elena was frightened and reacting in the only way she knew how.

"You want her to do it because you're sleeping with her. That doesn't mean she's any good as a surgeon. How do you know she can do the job? Or that Tony even needs surgery?"

She's scared, he repeated silently, and reined in his climbing temper. Putting his hands on her shoulders, he squeezed gently. "Elena, think. First off, Marissa is the head of trauma surgery, which ought to tell you something. And if that doesn't help, do you really believe I'd let anyone work on Tony who wasn't qualified? Who I wasn't positive would give him the best care possible? No matter what she was to me? This is Tony's life. Marissa's the best, Elena. Let her do her job."

She stared at him and then she crumpled, flinging herself against his chest and sobbing. "Don't let Tony die," she cried. "Please, don't let Tony die."

"He won't die." Jack held her, looked at Marissa over her head. "She's agreed. I'll take her to sign the papers."

"It's going to take a while," Marissa said. "Don't imagine the worst."

The elevator doors closed on his son and the woman he loved.

Jack and Elena didn't talk much. Both too afraid to give voice to their fears, Jack figured. As if by not talking about those fears, they could make them go away. It wasn't working.

At least Marissa was Tony's surgeon. Though Jack had been irritated by her doctor double-talk, he trusted her implicitly. He'd always admired her professionalism. Even before he knew her well, he'd known of her reputation for high standards and conscientious work. There was no one else he would have entrusted with his son's life.

Marissa had even handled Elena's hysterics and accusations with admirable composure. It didn't surprise him, but her reaction made him appreciate and respect her even more.

Elena broke the silence. "It's been so long. Why is it taking so long?"

He patted his pocket for the cigarettes that were no longer there. "I don't know. She said she'd—" He broke off, seeing Marissa walking swiftly toward them. Smiling. That could only mean Tony had made it. Jack stood, his heart beating fast with rising hope and lingering fear.

"Tony's on his way to recovery now," she said, stopping in front of them. "He came through the surgery very well."

Jack closed his eyes and offered up a silent prayer of thanks. A tidal wave of relief flooded through him.

"He's alive?" Elena choked out. "Alive?"

Taking her hand, Marissa said, "Very much so. As I suspected, it was a splenic laceration. We were able to repair the damage without removing the spleen. There were no other major organs involved. Tony should recover fully."

Jack put his arm around Elena, steadying her as she leaned against him, sobbing. "Thank you," he said, holding his hand out to Marissa. She clasped it, returning the hard squeeze he gave her. "I don't know what else to say."

She smiled again and shook her head. "You'll both want to see him, but remember, he's still under the anesthesia. It will be a little while before he wakes."

"Tony's really going to be all right?" Elena asked.

"If he progresses as I expect, with no complications, then he'll be good as new in a few weeks."

Elena shifted uncomfortably before she said, "I owe you an apology for what I said earlier. Thank you for—for what you did."

Surprised, Jack heard true gratitude in Elena's voice.

"No apologies necessary," Marissa said. "You were concerned about your son." Smiling wryly, she added, "Believe me, I've dealt with parents who gave me much more grief than you did."

"I'm going to see him now," Elena said, wiping at her eyes. "Are you coming, Jack?"

"In a minute. You go ahead, I want to talk to Marissa first."

"He's fine, Jack. Really," Marissa said as Elena left. She gave his hand another squeeze.

He pulled her into his arms and hugged her tightly. "You saved my son's life," he said against her hair.

"It could have been much worse. Tony was lucky."

"Lucky he had you for his doctor."

Her arms around him soothed him. "He's lucky he's got you. Go see him. You'll feel better once you do."

"Yeah." Jack framed her face in his hands. "I love you." He let go of her and walked to the doorway. Pausing, he looked back at Marissa. A lump formed in his throat. She looked so beautiful, standing there in bloody scrubs with strain still etched around her eyes. If only . . .

"Thank you," he said again, and left.

"What do you mean, Tony doesn't want to see me?" Standing just outside Tony's hospital room, Jack stared at Elena and Marissa. "He didn't say anything like that yesterday."

"Yesterday he was groggy," Elena told him. "He said it today. Just now."

She looked like she felt sorry for him. Pity? From Elena? What was she up to? "Is this your doing, Elena?"

"You know I've never kept you from Tony," she snapped. "Don't blame it on me. What did you do to him? Did you have a fight?"

Jack's gaze met Marissa's. "I need to talk to him. Whether he wants me to or not."

Compassion in her eyes and her voice, Marissa said, "I'm afraid you can't."

Two crude, succinct words expressed what he thought about that. Shoving past the two women, he put his hand on the door. "I'm going in there to see my son. If he doesn't want me, he can tell me himself."

"Jack." Marissa placed a restraining hand on his chest. "Wait, don't do this. Tony became very agitated when Elena tried to talk to him about seeing you. He was adamant that he didn't want to see you."

"That's crazy. He doesn't mean it. He can't."

Marissa's hand felt firm and determined. Jack could have easily flung it off, but something stopped him. Maybe the fact that it was Marissa holding him back.

"I'm sorry, Jack, but he does mean it. Don't force me to call security. Think about Tony, about what's best for him. He's just had surgery."

"You'd call security on me?" He didn't need to hear her answer; he knew it even as he asked the question.

"If I have to. Tony is my patient and I intend to do everything I can to assure his recovery."

His chest hurt. An odd numbness, a feeling of unreality overtook him. Furiously, Jack shoved himself away from the door and paced. "Why?" he demanded. "Why would he suddenly decide he didn't want to see me?"

Marissa and Elena exchanged glances. "We don't know," Marissa said. "He wouldn't tell either of us. Tony's in a fragile physical state right now. His emotional state is just as precarious. It wouldn't be in his best interest to disregard his feelings."

"Not in his best interests," Jack repeated. How could it *not* be in Tony's best interests to see his father? None of this made sense. Unbelieving, he stared at Marissa. She gazed back, steady, compassionate—and determined. He'd seen that look before. Her turf. He'd lose this fight.

Turning away, he asked Elena, "What did he say? Didn't he give you some kind of reason?"

Elena shook her head. "No, nothing. He said to tell you to stay away from him." Hesitantly, she placed a hand on his arm. "Honestly, Jack, I'm sorry."

His stomach hurt like he'd been kicked hard in the gut. He waited until she'd left before he spoke to Marissa. "Tony's reacting to you and me, isn't he? That's what this is about. Some crazy idea—I never imagined he'd take it this way."

Marissa frowned. "We don't know that for certain. I told you, he wouldn't say why."

Jack rammed his fingers through his hair. "Seems pretty damn clear to me. I tell him I'm thinking of getting married again and wham, bam, the next thing I know he's in the hospital, nearly dead."

"Don't, Jack. Tony made a poor decision. That isn't your fault."

Frustrated, hurt, he jammed his hands in his jacket pockets. "Yes, it is. Don't sugarcoat it, Marissa." Every bit of it was his fault—and there was nothing he could do about it because Tony wouldn't even see him. Like his sister hadn't listened to him.

"He'll change his mind. Give him a little time."

"Right. Like I have a choice." Whirling, he strode away from her. "I'm going to the station. Call me if . . . Call me."

"You should get some sleep."

"Can't. I've got something cooking on the Phoenix case."

God knows, he didn't look forward to finding out the truth about Burt King, but it was something he had to face. Just like he had to face the fact that his son refused to see him. How had it happened? And why?

"Why the mysterious phone call?" King asked, taking a seat in Jack's office. Huffing from the effort, he added, "I got here as soon as I could. Your sergeant said it was urgent."

"It is," Jack said, fighting an urge to puke. He let King consider his response for a long moment, then said, "You're going down, Burt."

Though King stared at him blankly, Jack didn't miss the flash of fear in his eyes. His ruddy face paled, the gray of his hair accenting his pallor.

"Going down? What are you talking about, Corelli? Going down for what?"

"See this?" Jack tapped the manila folder on his desk. "Photos, bank-account receipts, all kinds of interesting little items here. Your record didn't stand up to a full-scale investigation. You should have known it wouldn't." He crumpled a piece of paper. "Crash, burn." He dropped the paper in the trash can. "You're busted."

"What kind of crap are you spouting?" King blustered, tightly gripping the arms of the chair. "I can have your badge for this, Corelli."

"No, I don't think so. To do that you'll have to be acquitted, and that isn't going to happen. We've got so much on you, I can take my pick of charges. But there's no contest. Murder one will work, won't it?"

"Murder?" King drew his breath in with an audible hiss. "What the hell are you talking about? You're crazy."

Watching him squirm, Jack narrowed his eyes and grimaced. "Yeah, you got that right. This makes me crazy. A dirty cop's bad enough, but a dirty cop who's a cop killer—that's unconscionable." Jack waited a beat and added, "Wonder how long you'll last in the pen."

King had gone totally white now. Sweat beaded on

his forehead. "Cop killer? Are you saying . . . I don't know where you dreamed this up, but—"

"Not a dream, King. An eyewitness account placing you at Roth's safe house the night he and his guards were murdered pretty much toasts your buns. Those guards trusted you, you sorry pile of crap, and you shot them down like dogs. Broadhurst was one of them, one of ours. He left behind a wife and a baby. And a lot of cops who'd love to see whoever killed him get his."

"Who?" King whispered. "The witness . . ."

Jack laughed harshly. "Oh, no. This is one witness you won't find. That witness is buried deep and won't come ˙out until your trial. You've made your last mistake."

The former captain hid his face in his hands and sat silently for several minutes. Jack said nothing, watching him self-destruct.

"What—what do you want?" King finally choked out.

"Let's make a deal, huh?" Sickened, Jack wondered what had happened to the man he thought he knew. "God, you're piled so high with stink, I'm not sure I can go through with this. You know, as much as all this makes me sick, I could've dealt with it. But you used me. You used me, you son-of-a-bitch, to get to Roth, to go after Marissa. Was I next on your list? Just how stupid, how blind do you think I am? Did you think to use me to set up my own murder?"

"No!" Agonized, King looked up. "Jack, you don't understand. I had to do it, he gave me no choice."

"Save it for the bleeding hearts," he said, cutting him off with a slash of his hand. "I'm not one of them. There's always a choice. You made yours the day you pocketed that first bribe and turned it into a diamond bracelet to buy yourself a gold digger."

His eyes wild, King shouted, "I had to! She wouldn't have stayed with me! I needed her . . . had to have her. She—she made me feel like a man again."

Disgust settled in the pit of Jack's stomach like a cold ball of lead. "You're not a man, you're a whipped mongrel. No." He held up a hand. "Don't tell me any more. I don't want your justification. I don't want to hear why or how—tell it to your lawyer. Maybe he can stomach it, because I sure as hell can't."

King crumbled so fast, it was pathetic. "A deal, you said a deal. I can give you names, addresses, dates—"

"The Phoenix. I want him."

"Phoenix?" King stared at him blankly. "The boss? His name? You want me to name the Phoenix?"

"Name him. And bring him down."

"Set him up?"

"Catch on real fast, don't you? Yeah, I want to set up a sting. And you're going to bring the guest of honor."

"If something goes wrong—"

"If something goes wrong, you'll be the first to go. Remember that and make sure nothing does. No last-minute double cross. The name, King. I want the name."

For the first time since he'd walked in, King met Jack's gaze. "Paxton Welch."

Blood roared in Jake's ears, rage filled his soul. He had suspected, maybe even known it, but hearing it confirmed added to his soul-deep sickness. His son had practically been living with the bastard. God knows what harm he'd caused Tony. Could Tony's gang involvement be traced to Welch?

Jack whipped around his desk, grabbed the front of King's shirt, and hauled him up, shaking him like a dog with a rat. "You knew Welch was involved with Elena. You knew Tony would be around him, and you did nothing." Viciously, he shook him again. "Said nothing. I ought to kill you for that alone."

"Welch would have killed me! There was nothing I could do! I couldn't help it—"

"Shut up," Jack said, throwing him back in the chair and closing his eyes for a moment. "Just shut up." If he stayed there much longer, he knew his hands would go around King's throat. Regaining control, he called Gabe in.

With a gesture at King, Jack said, "He's agreed to deliver the Phoenix. Set it up." Jack put a hand on his belly, willing it to settle. Throughout his career, he'd been sickened by many things. This was the worst. "I've got to get out of here. Can you handle things?"

"Yes, sir."

"Put someone on him twenty-four hours. Make this quick. I want that ring broken, the sooner the better. You can reach me by beeper if you need me."

"Yes, sir," Gabe said again.

Jack looked at what had once been a good cop, a decent man. "How do you live with yourself, Burt?"

King didn't answer.

ELEVEN

Why couldn't they leave him alone? Tony thought. He'd told them a hundred times he wasn't going to see his dad and here sat Marissa ready to start in on him again. His mom had finally given up, why wouldn't she?

The truth was, he missed his dad. Missed talking to him, missed being with him. He wished he didn't miss him. He wished they hadn't lied to him.

"You'll be out of here in a few days," Marissa was saying. "Are you finally going to see your dad then?"

"No." Tony shot her a dirty look, then glanced away.

"Don't you think you should tell him why?"

"What difference does it make? He'll just—" He stopped, fighting back tears. What did she care, anyway?

Marissa gave him a few minutes before she spoke again. "Did you know that if you tell me something in confidence, I can't repeat it? Not to your father, not to your mother, not to anyone."

Distrustfully, he looked at her. Yeah, right. He'd heard *that* before. "Why can't you?"

"Because you're my patient. It's called doctor-patient confidentiality. Whatever you tell me stays between us—just like the psychiatrist can't talk about your sessions with her."

"Yeah, she told me, but I don't care. She's a dweeb."

"Your psychiatrist is a dweeb?" Marissa looked like she was trying not to laugh.

He shrugged. "Yeah. So?"

"I'm sorry you don't feel like you can talk to her. But as your doctor, I'm advising you to talk. To someone. Keeping everything inside as a way to protect yourself can backfire on you, Tony. I've done it enough to know."

Oh, right, he thought. She didn't look like she'd ever had a problem in her life. What did she know about parents and their lies?

"You can ask for a different psychiatrist," she went on. "Or you can talk to me. Of course, you might think I'm a dweeb, too, but I'm still ready to listen. I'd like to help you, Tony, if you'll let me."

No, she wasn't a dweeb. If she weren't trying to take his dad away from him, he'd probably like her a lot. The anger boiling inside him wanted out bad. It was *her* fault too. "Why should I talk to you? Why do you care? What's it to you whether I see him or not?"

"I care because you're my patient. When you're emotionally upset it hinders your healing." She smiled and added, "And I care because I'm in love with your father, and you're very important to him. He loves you a lot, so I figure you must be pretty special."

"Right," he said with a hollow laugh. "You'll like it

better if I'm not around. Then you can have him to yourself. You're a liar, just like he is. Like my mom is. You're all lying."

"Lying about what, Tony?"

The words burst out of him, hot and tortured. "He's not my dad! He's not my dad and he's been lying about it my whole stinking life!"

She stared at him, looking as shocked as he'd felt when he had first heard. But that had to be a lie too.

"What do you mean, he's not your dad?"

Once the dam had burst, it all poured out. "My mom and that slimeball Welch—I heard them talking. They said I wasn't Jack's 'natural' son, so if he married you he might have a kid of his 'own.' Don't you get it? *She* lied too. They're both liars." Fury and jealousy in his heart, he glared at her. "Just like you're a liar. You knew, didn't you?" Tony clenched his fists into the sheet on the bed. "Sure you did. He told you, but he wouldn't tell me." Biting his lip, he waited for her answer.

She touched his arm. "Tony, he hasn't ever said a word to me about it."

Suspiciously, he studied her. He wanted to believe her, but he couldn't. "Sure, right. Who cares?"

"Don't you think you owe it to your father to ask him? Give him a chance to explain it? Maybe you misunderstood, or misinterpreted what your mother said."

"No. That's what they said. And my mom said, 'Tony doesn't know. I don't want him to hear.'" He blinked back tears. "I was so dumb, I never even wondered why I don't look like him. Never even . . . thought about it."

"Have you asked your mother about this? After all, she's the one you overheard."

That was a laugh. "Mom would flip out. Besides, she—" He hesitated, then decided it didn't matter. "She lies all the time. And now I know they *both* lie."

Frowning, Marissa spoke slowly. "Okay, let's say it's true. You think because he adopted you, that means your father doesn't love you?"

"He lied. If he lied about adopting me, he could lie about other stuff too."

"Maybe he had a good reason for not telling you. Ask him. Give him a chance."

Tony didn't answer because he didn't know what to say. He didn't understand why, but talking to Marissa eased the tightness in his chest. It shouldn't have mattered, but it did. She didn't treat him like a kid, she treated him like a person. The way his dad had before . . . before Tony had found out the truth.

"Do you think," she asked, "that you have to be your father's biological son for him to love you?"

Haltingly, he tried to explain. "It—it's not the same. Being adopted, well, it's just *different*. When—if you have a kid, then he won't want me. He won't need me, he'll have a kid of his own. His *real* kid."

Marissa leaned forward and tapped his bed. "You're jumping to a lot of conclusions. We may not even get married. We may not have any children if we do get married. Nothing is settled yet."

"But—"

"That's not the point, though, is it?" she interrupted. "You're angry because your parents didn't tell you that your father adopted you. So now you've decided that Jack is just marking time with you until something—someone—better comes along."

It sounded stupid when she put it that way. "I guess," he said, striving for the defiance that had been inside him for weeks but was fading now.

"Before you found out, did you have any complaints with how your father treated you? Did he ignore you or not do the things you asked him to? Did he treat you badly?"

"Well, no, but—"

"Could you depend on him? Would he talk to you and be there for you?"

He'd never thought about that part of it. Depend on his dad? "Yeah," he admitted in a low voice.

Marissa stood and put her hand on his arm. Her touch was cool, soothing. Again, though it made him feel better, he didn't know why. Maybe it was the doctor thing.

"Then he is your father, Tony, blood or not. Because blood isn't the important thing—love is. It's not difficult to father a child. Staying around, loving him, caring for him, being there for him, that's hard. But you need to figure that out for yourself."

Her eyes grew cloudy. Though she looked at him, Tony didn't think she saw him anymore.

"I'm not adopted," she went on, "but I used to wish I could be. My biological father never stuck around, never loved me, was never someone I could depend on. After my mother died, he dragged me around the country with him, dumping me on anyone he could find while he went off to another new adventure. Dear old Dad might have fathered me, but he wasn't a *father*. That's the difference between my dad and yours."

Tony waited until she reached the door before he spoke. "You're really not going to tell him?"

She turned around to look at him. "I can't repeat what you told me. But even if I could, I wouldn't. This is between you and your parents, Tony. You need to be the one to tell them, not me."

After she left, he realized she hadn't done any of the things he thought she'd do. Not even make him promise to think about seeing his dad and talking to him. She hadn't needed to. Tony knew he wouldn't think of anything else.

Marissa had never been tempted to break a confidence before, particularly a professional one. But she'd never seen Jack look as miserable as he did when he came in that night. If only she could help him, at least give him a glimmer of hope. But she couldn't.

"Tony?" he asked.

The hope faded from his eyes when she shook her head. "I'm sorry."

"Yeah, well, it goes with the day I've had," he said, and headed for the kitchen.

She heard him rummaging around. "Are you hungry?"

"Nope." He walked out holding a nearly full bottle of Jack Daniel's and a glass half-filled with ice cubes.

Surprised, she raised her eyebrows. Since he'd moved in with her, she'd never seen him have more than an occasional beer. "That bad?"

He poured deliberately, raised his glass, and drank deeply before answering her. "Guess you could say I'm celebrating."

Something was wrong, something more than Tony. Marissa wanted to comfort him, but he didn't look like he wanted comfort. She wasn't sure what he wanted. "What happened?"

His laugh, as well as his expression, was harsh. He settled himself on the couch and propped his feet on the coffee table. "We've got the Phoenix. Or we will have him. The case should be wrapped up tighter than a Christmas present in a day or two. All we need is for the sting to work and we've got him."

"Isn't that what you wanted?"

"Careful what you ask for," he said enigmatically. "Want to hear something funny? The Phoenix has been right under my nose for months. Practically living with my ex-wife. And my son. Nice, huh?"

Living with . . . "Welch? Paxton Welch is the Phoenix?" Though she'd never liked him, she couldn't imagine him as an organized-crime boss.

"Number one of the whole shebang." In a different tone, detached and eerily matter-of-fact, he added, "I wonder if I can bring him in."

Startled, she asked, "What do you mean? Why couldn't you? Aren't you going to have the evidence to arrest him?"

His eyes changed swiftly, from detached to dark and angry. "Evidence shouldn't be a problem. The problem is me. I don't want to bring him in." He paused, and a heartbeat of tension filled the room. "I want to kill him."

She heard the truth of it in his voice, flat, emotionless. Read the truth in his eyes, hostile, bitter.

But however he felt, she knew Jack. "You won't, though. Not unless you have to."

His gaze locked with hers. "You think I won't? Why not? Why the hell shouldn't I?"

"Because you're a cop. A good cop, a conscientious cop. It's not in you, Jack." If she knew nothing else about him, she knew that.

Softly, slowly, he said, "Isn't it? I'm not so sure of that. For the first time since I became a cop, I'm not sure. About anything."

"I am."

He shoved her words aside with a shake of his head. "Know how we got him? A dirty cop gave him up. A stinking, murdering, dirty *cop*."

"Someone you know." His mood, his demeanor, made that obvious.

Another swig, a nod. "You got it. The retired chief of juvenile. Burt King."

King. The name was familiar, but it took her a minute to place it. "Wasn't he—didn't you say he was the one who helped you when you were a teenager?"

"Good memory, Doc." He toasted her, swallowed the rest, and refilled his glass.

His words weren't slurred yet, but at the rate he was drinking it wouldn't take long.

Thinking about her own life, she said, "It . . . hurts when someone you trust lets you down."

"Do me a favor and don't spout any psychiatric crap. I'm not in the mood."

Her anger was much easier to control than the hurt. "All right. What are you in the mood for?"

"Getting drunk," he said. "How about you? Care to join me?" He waved the bottle in the air. "Plenty for both of us."

"Thanks, I'll pass." She sat beside him and waited for more.

"Don't look at me like that, either," he snarled, and tossed back another swallow.

"How am I looking at you?"

"With your compassionate doctor look. I don't like it and I don't need it. Take it someplace else, Doc."

She studied him for a long moment before she spoke. "Are you that desperate to fight? Or just desperate to forget what's bothering you?"

He gave her a sour look. "I'm not desperate." His fingers tightened around the glass. Clenched so tight, she could see the whitened knuckles.

"And I won't fight," she told him. Again, she wanted to comfort, but she wasn't sure how.

Jack set his glass down and raked his hand through his hair. "Seems like the least you could do," he muttered in a disgusted tone.

"Sorry," she said, smiling.

"You never do what I expect."

They were silent a moment. Then Marissa spoke. "I know people always say they know how you feel, but I think I do." Though Jack sent her a skeptical look, he didn't interrupt. "When I was sixteen I finally realized that you can't depend on the people you love. I should have known it long before that, but back then I was a slow learner."

"Your old man."

"That's right, my father. It was my sixteenth birthday. He swore he'd be there. That he'd take me to get my driver's license and then we'd celebrate. And he'd let me drive his new car. I'd been driving, racing, actually, for a couple of years. It gave him an ego boost to teach me and I was so pathetically grateful for any crumbs he gave me. Of course, he didn't show up. A woman, a race—I don't even remember the reason, except that he left town and didn't bother to tell me."

"Marissa—"

"I'm not finished," she interrupted, stamping down on the pain the memories brought. "By then he had the money to pay someone to stay with me. That night I took her car out and wrapped it around a telephone pole. I spent the next three months in the hospital. My father didn't bother to show up until a week after the accident." She was silent for a moment, then added, "That was when I decided to go into medicine. The hospital staff gave me more compassion and caring than my own father."

Jack didn't say anything. He pulled her into his arms and laid her head on his shoulder. His hand stroked over her hair, gently, comfortingly. "He didn't deserve you," he murmured.

"When he finally dragged himself in to see me, he said he'd stayed away because he felt guilty, but I knew better." It was because he hadn't cared. Jack's arms tightened around her, holding her close. Against his heart. Nobody had held her before when she hurt. Jack was the only person who had ever cared enough to hold her, to be there, to share her pain. She had started out to comfort him, and instead, he was comforting her. He'd triggered memories and feelings she hadn't realized lay so close to the surface.

"You'll get through it," she told him, hoping it was true.

"We'll both get through it," he said.

But would they come through it together? she wondered.

God, he was jumpy. Whenever a big sting went
down, Jack got jumpy, but this time was worse than
usual. Gabe had moved fast setting up the sting. Now,
the evening of the day after they'd busted King, everything was set and ready to go.

The location had been prepared, King had been
wired, briefed, and was supposedly eager to help them
reel in Paxton Welch. Jack didn't trust him, though. In
his experience, dirty cops rarely cleaned up again. And
King was not only dirty, he'd killed a fellow cop. Jack
wouldn't trust him now from here to the mailbox. In
Jack's opinion, the only thing King really wanted was to
save his butt any way he could. So he intended to keep a
real close eye on Burt King.

The abandoned pipe warehouse, a place King had
assured them he'd used before to meet with Welch, still
held odors of the last rave party held there. Sex, drugs,
and techno music—today's youth played dangerous
games, Jack mused. Rave parties were so dangerous, the
police department had learned from tragic experience
that it was better to wait outside and pick up stragglers
than try to bust one. The Phoenix ring had long been
suspected of providing different locations as well as
drugs for the parties.

Hell of a spot for a party, Jack thought, his gaze
taking in the sheer size of the warehouse. He stepped
over a fallen I beam, searching for a likely hiding place.
On the other side of the huge room, Gabe and his half
of the team did the same thing.

The place displayed an odd mixture of its original use and its more recent one. Broken glass and beer cans lay amid rusty pipes of varying sizes. Drug paraphernalia lay strewn in one corner—slivers of broken mirrors, razor blades, straws. In another lay a huge pile of ancient nuts and bolts, as rusted as the pipes. A broken-down forklift sat forlornly off to one side, a dejected metal dinosaur that had outlived its usefulness.

Gabe's men had secreted themselves for the most part behind huge drums, empty now, which had once held machine oil or gasoline. Jack's part of the team was no longer in sight, either. Choosing a place as close to King as possible, Jack concealed himself behind a stack of pipes and barrels, drew his gun, and sat down to wait.

His every muscle was tensed and ready to spring, and he wondered if Welch would be on time. He wished he had Marissa's faith in him. Though he'd spent most of the night thinking about it, he still wasn't absolutely certain he could maintain his professionalism. Not with Welch.

The bastard had used Tony. Even if he hadn't known to start with, once the lawyer found out Tony had been busted for burglary, he would have known the kid had gotten in with one of the very gangs Phoenix controlled. The thought made Jack's blood hum and his anger sizzle, primed to explode.

Deliberately, Jack turned his thoughts from Tony and concentrated on the problem at hand. Could King get Welch to admit to ordering Roth's murder? That would be the key, because he didn't trust the legal system with Welch involved. The slick lawyer would have many ways to twist and maneuver his way out of an indictment, but a taped confession would spike his guns just dandy.

The garagelike metal door squealed, slowly rolling upward. Welch. Jack's free hand curled into a fist as he concentrated on not stepping out from behind the barrels and simply blowing the bastard away. When he thought about the misery Phoenix had caused, not just to Tony but to so many young lives, it was almost more than he could handle. But he was a cop, so he dealt with it.

"What the hell do you mean dragging me out here?" Welch asked King, his normally cultured tone slipping into a harsher street version. "I've told you a thousand times never to call me. Have you gone senile? Or are you just stupid?"

"This is important, or I wouldn't have called," King said, his voice sounding tense and tinny coming over the wire. "Corelli's onto something. I'm in trouble and you're going to have to help me."

"Corelli couldn't find his own butt with a map," Welch said.

Jack smiled, picturing the bastard's face when he arrested him.

"If you're in trouble," Welch added, "that's your problem, not mine."

"He's close. My sources say he might have tied you to the Roth murder."

Welch snorted. "Nobody can tie me to a damn thing. You're the murderer, King, not me."

"You ordered it."

Welch's laugh sounded genuinely amused. "Where's your proof? You think anyone will take the word of a crooked cop over that of an upstanding citizen like myself?" He laughed again. "You're a riot, old man."

From his position, Gabe looked at Jack expectantly, waiting for the signal to move in, but Jack didn't give it. Close, he thought, but no cigar. Jack wanted the cigar—a confession, a straight-out admission of guilt. *Come on, Burt, prove there's still something left of the cop I used to know.*

King's voice dropped low, so that Jack had to strain to hear.

"I'm telling you, Corelli's *close*. Understand? He's ready to blow the Phoenix ring wide open. He's damned *close*."

Son-of-a-bitch! It hit Jack like a load of bricks dropped on his chest. *He's pulling a double cross, tipping the bastard off.* Out of time, Jack signaled to Gabe to move.

TWELVE

Marissa went about her work as usual the next day, but she couldn't stop her thoughts from drifting to Jack. To what he'd told her was going to happen soon. A sting. How dangerous was that? Could he be hurt, even killed? *Of course he could, you idiot. He's a cop.* Quickly, she shut off the image of Jack, covered in blood, being wheeled into the hospital.

What was the matter with her? It wasn't like her to imagine disasters. She saw enough of the real thing without having to resort to nightmare illusions. Jack was a good cop, he could take care of himself. But she couldn't quite shake the nagging fear that something would go wrong with their plans to arrest the Phoenix.

When she made rounds late that afternoon, she found Tony just hanging up the phone. "I won't be long," she told him. "Sorry you had to cut your call short."

He shrugged and didn't answer. Marissa read his chart, scribbled a few instructions, and started to leave. She saw no point in trying to talk to him again. If their discussion the day before hadn't made him reconsider seeing his father, she doubted anything she could add now would make a difference.

"Wait," Tony said.

At the door, she looked over her shoulder at him. "Yes?"

Gnawing his lip, he looked troubled, unde-cided—and young.

"Do you know where my dad is?" he asked at last.

A wave of hope swept through her, though she an-swered him matter-of-factly. "Have you tried the sta-tion?"

Tony nodded. "Yeah. He's not there and they won't tell me where he is. I tried his car too. Do you know where he is?" he repeated.

Could Jack have set up the operation to trap Phoe-nix already? she wondered. He had said he expected the case to be wrapped up shortly, within a couple of days. "Not for certain," she answered. "Did you call his beeper number?"

"He doesn't like me to do that unless it's really im-portant."

Amused, she smiled. "I have a hunch he'll consider talking to you important enough to warrant paging him."

"Maybe." Somberly, Tony looked at her. "Do you really think so?"

"No doubt about it. Call him."

Marissa watched him place the call and key in his number. She hated to leave before Jack returned the call, but she had to finish rounds. "I'll check on you a little later, okay?"

Tony merely rolled a shoulder, but she thought he looked pleased.

Later, when she returned, he didn't look pleased anymore. Sullen was more the word. "You didn't get him?"

"Nah."

His attempt at indifference failed miserably. Oh, Jack, she thought, why did you have to be gone *now?* "Tony, he's on a big case. Last night he told me something might break on it any time. I'm sure he'll call or come by as soon as he's able to."

"Right."

"Your father asks about you every time I see him or talk to him. Believe me, he wants to see you more than he wants anything."

"I'm tired," he said, trying to dismiss her.

"You've come this far. You made the first step, the hardest one, when you called him. Don't give up now."

Marissa stayed for a few more minutes, but Tony was obviously tapped out. He closed his eyes, feigning sleep to get her to leave, she suspected. Shortly, he was asleep in fact.

Whatever you're doing, Jack, she thought, I hope you finish soon. Resolutely, she tried to ignore the uneasy feelings she'd had since the night before, since he'd told her about King and Welch. Jack was a good cop. She wouldn't let her suddenly wild imagination take control.

At one A.M. Jack walked in the door of Marissa's apartment. The fear that had simmered all day in the back of her mind erupted into sheer terror at the sight of him. Blood smeared his cheek, saturated his shirt, splattered his jeans.

"Oh, my God," she whispered, staring at him, unable to move. Then her training took over and she began snapping orders. "Lie down, let me examine you. Hank, call the hospital, tell them we're on our way. Why are you walking around like this?" she demanded of Jack. "Why aren't you already at the hosp—"

He caught her hands and held them. "Marissa, it's not my blood. I'm okay."

Her hands stilled, halting the rapid examination she'd begun. "Not yours?"

He shook his head. "No. I didn't mean to scare you."

"You're really not hurt?"

"Not a scratch."

"Good." She closed her eyes and willed her heart to calm its frenetic beating. Opening them, she said, "Now I can kill you with a clear conscience. Don't ever do that to me again. My God, I thought—"

He cut her off, kissing her, good and hard, on her mouth. When she would have spoken, he kissed her again.

Hank cleared his throat loudly. "What happened?"

Jack broke the kiss, brushing his hand over her cheek before he looked at his partner. "Welch is in custody. King's dead. Natterhorn took a bullet, but he's okay."

"Anyone else hurt?"

Jack eased his arm across Marissa's shoulders. "No, thank God. We got lucky there. King tried to tip Welch off. It wasn't pretty, but it could have been worse. At least Phoenix is blown wide open now."

"Nothing about this case has been easy," Hank said. "The main thing is, you took Phoenix down." He and Jack shook hands.

Marissa felt the bond between the two men. Cop to cop, partner to partner, expressed in the duration of a handshake.

"I'll catch the details tomorrow," Hank said.

"Yeah, tomorrow." Jack shut the door behind him. "I'm going to shower," he said. He was at the bathroom door when she spoke.

"Tony tried to call you."

Turning, he stared at her, a stunned expression on his face. "Tony? He wants to talk to me?"

"He tried to get you all afternoon and evening."

"Dammit! The one time I wasn't there."

"I told him that you were on a big case. That you'd come see him as soon as you could."

Jack glanced at his watch and shook his head. "No sense getting him up now. It'll have to wait until morning." As he shut the bathroom door she heard him mutter, "Just my luck."

A short while later he came out, pulling his FWPD sweatshirt over his head. He looked exhausted and despondent, but at least he wasn't covered in blood any longer.

"What happened tonight, Jack? Whose blood was that?"

Wearily, he threw himself down beside her on the couch. "King's, mostly. Welch—" He closed his eyes and opened them again. "King tried to tip Welch off. When we went in, Welch shot Gabe. I took a shot at Welch. The bastard made sure I got Burt instead."

Oh, Lord, what had that done to him? "Are you all right?"

Bleakly, he looked at her. "No. I'm about as far from all right as I can get. Burt died by my hand." Jack looked at his hand and repeated, "By my hand. He was dirty, he was double-crossing me, but dammit, I didn't want to be the one to kill him."

Marissa smoothed her hand over his brow. "I wish I could help you. Make things better for you."

"Do you?" His gaze locked with hers.

A loaded question, she thought, though she wasn't sure why.

"Tell me you'll marry me," he said. "Quit making me wonder if it's ever going to happen and just . . . tell it to me straight."

"Why are you bringing this up now? Do we have to—"

"Yeah, I do have to. I have to know, Marissa."

Her heart ached for him. Jack needed a commitment—the one thing she couldn't give to him. Marissa would have given anything not to have to talk about marriage just then. She didn't want to hurt him again, and she knew she would. "I can't give you an answer now. Not the one you want."

"Why?"

It was a simple question and he deserved an answer, even if she wasn't sure how to explain. She didn't fully understand it herself. "I've been making my own decisions for a long time. It would be hard—no impossible, for me to let you take control. I won't do it, Jack. I can't."

"Marissa, I want to share your life, not control it."

"How can you say that? You've been taking decisions out of my hands since the day Juju Jerome took me hostage."

"That's crap," he shot back. "Was I in control when you kept working? Hell no, I wanted you in a safe house. And what about after that? If I had my way, you'd still be in the safe house. Instead you're a sitting duck for Jerome."

"You had no choice in the matter. That's why—"

He cut her off. "I had plenty of choice. This control thing might be part of why you're scared to commit to me, but I think I know the real reason. You're positive that I'll let you down, like your father did. Like your ex-husband did. That just because I say I love you today doesn't mean I'll love you tomorrow. Or the day after. But you're wrong, Marissa, even if I can't prove it to you."

Was he right? she asked herself, staring at him. Was it as simple as that? Was she afraid to open herself up to the pain again? She didn't know. She truly didn't know.

You really blew it this time, Corelli. Jack lay in bed and cursed himself for ever bringing up the subject of marriage. He should have known better than to try to back Marissa into a corner. He'd only made her more certain that their marriage would never work.

The phone rang. Knowing she wasn't on call, he reached across her sleeping body and grabbed it. "Corelli."

"Dad?"

"Tony?" Instantly alert, he sat up.

"Dad, I'm scared. I woke up and he was just sitting

here, in my room. He says—" Abruptly, his voice cut off, but not before Jack recognized the raw fear in it.

"Tony! Tony, what's wrong? Who's there?"

"Your son can't come to the phone right now, Corelli. He's puking all over the nice, clean hospital floor. You'd think he never saw a gun before."

Pure, unadulterated fear slammed a hammer fist into his belly. Juju Jerome. Oh, God, Jerome had Tony. "Don't hurt him. If you touch him, Jerome, I swear I'll—"

"No threats," Jerome hissed. "I'm in charge this time, Corelli."

"What do you want? Name it, I'll do it."

Jerome's laugh crawled up Jack's spine and lodged a ball of terror in his mind. That laugh promised no mercy, it promised revenge. Why Tony? Why hadn't he thought to put a guard on his son? He should have—and now his mistake could cost Tony his life.

"The bitch," Jerome said, "that's what I want. Give me blondie and you get your boy back. Alive. As long as no cops come nosing around in the meantime. Don't try none of that SWAT-team jive with me, neither. If I hear any negotiation BS, the kid's dead. Let me even *smell* another cop besides you, and the angels come for the kid."

He felt Marissa move, awake now and sitting up in bed staring at him. A choice. His son's life or the woman he loved. He couldn't give up either one. "No," he told Jerome. "Anything else. If you want a hostage, take me. I'll get you out of the country. You can disappear, you'll never have to come back—"

"No deal, cop. I don't want you, I don't want 'anything else.' The bitch for the kid. Tell blondie I'm waiting for her."

The line went dead. Jack's heart slammed a desperate beat in his chest.

His gaze met Marissa's. "Jerome's got Tony."

Her eyes widened with horror. "Oh, God. What does he want?"

Jack couldn't speak. He looked at her and his throat closed tight. "I've got to go," he finally said, jumping out of bed and grabbing for his clothes.

"Say it, Jack. He wants *me*, doesn't he?" Her voice was quiet, and dead certain in tone.

Useless to deny the truth. "Forget it. I'll take care of everything." He had to.

She ignored him and began to pull on clothes. "You have to let me go, Jack. It's the only way to save Tony."

"The hell it is!" Impotent rage made him slam his fist against the wall. "I won't risk you. Do you hear me?"

"What about your son? Are you willing to risk him?"

Fighting his temper, his terror, he rubbed a hand over his face, waiting a moment before he spoke. "You can come to the hospital, but you're not going in that room. I'll take care of Tony."

"How?"

As Marissa drove to the hospital Jack asked himself that same question again and again. He hoped driving would keep her occupied long enough that she couldn't argue with him.

His first instinct had been to call in a SWAT team, but even if Jerome hadn't been so specific, he'd have thought long and hard before he did that. Sometimes

SWAT negotiations worked. Too often they failed. Jack had witnessed too many failures to take the chance with his own son as the hostage.

Using his cellular phone, he started to call Gabe before he remembered the man was injured. Instead, he called Hank, briefing him and stressing the need for absolute silence. One siren and Tony would die.

When he finished, Jack looked over at Marissa. She was driving one-handed, digging in her purse with the other.

"What the hell are you doing?"

Ignoring him, she kept right on, flinging items out as she searched. "Yes!" she said, drawing her hand out.

A short, cylindrical object lay in her palm. He stared at it in disbelief. "Pepper spray? When did you get that?"

"After you let me out of the safe house. You pitched such a fit about my not having any, Hank brought me several."

Stupidly, he had imagined that her silence during the drive meant she'd reconsidered. He should have known better, especially since he'd yet to win an argument with her. "Let me get this straight. You're planning to walk in the room with a killer using your handy-dandy *pepper spray* as a defense? That maniac has a gun, Marissa. What if you miss? Are you out of your mind?"

"Do you have a better idea?"

He didn't. "Holy Mother of God, I don't believe this." No time to waffle, no time to think. Only time to make up his mind.

Marissa pulled into the fire lane in front of the hospital. "We need a plan," she said, cutting the engine.

"Wrong. *I* need a plan. You don't come into it."

"Jack, Tony's in this mess because of me." Her voice was firm, persuasive. "Because Jerome wants *me.*"

Jack shook his head. "He's using Tony to manipulate me. It's my fault, I should have put a guard on him."

"That doesn't matter now. It's going to take both of us to outsmart Jerome. There's no other way—not and still keep Tony alive."

Jack started to curse at her, to forbid her to go anywhere near Juju Jerome. She was right, though. God help them, she was right. "Dammit to hell, what choice do I have?"

Every fiber, every instinct he had urged him to tell her no. Could he actually be considering letting Marissa put herself in that kind of danger? Allowing her to face a homicidal maniac *by herself*?

She laid her hand on his arm and locked gazes with him. "You don't have a choice. This is my decision, Jack. My choice. Let me help."

Subconsciously, he must have known all along that it would come to this. A plan came out of his mouth in the next instant.

"Try to get Jerome away from Tony before you spray him. The bastard's probably sitting right next to the bed, holding his gun on him. If you can't get him to move you'll have to go for it anyway. For God's sake, don't let that stuff get into your own eyes."

"No, I know. I've seen people in the ER who've been sprayed."

"Don't take your eyes off that gun, either. He *should* drop the gun and scream like a son-of-a-bitch. But that's not a guarantee, especially if you don't get him dead on. As soon as you spray him, yell like hell. I'll be in there the instant I hear you."

"It sounds so simple."

"We don't have time for complex."

THIRTEEN

Marissa's worst nightmare waited for her on the other side of the door. No choice. She'd told Jack he had no choice. But she had no choice, either. Even if she hadn't known Tony, even if he had meant nothing to her, even if he hadn't been Jack's son, she would still have had no choice. She could never allow an innocent to suffer for something that was ultimately her responsibility.

Juju Jerome wanted revenge. On her. To Jerome, Tony was merely a pawn. And she knew full well that pawns were expendable to people like Juju Jerome. More to the point, everyone was expendable to people like him. She drew in a deep breath and placed her hand on the door, willing her accustomed calm to take hold.

"Marissa." Jack's voice halted her. His hand closed around her upper arm, dragging her away from the door. "God, I can't believe I'm letting you do this. It's insane. *I'm* insane to even consider it." His eyes were dark, intense.

"No, you're not," she said. "I'm choosing to do it. You respect me enough to let me make my own decision. You trust me, and yourself, enough to know that this is the only possible decision either of us can make."

The realization of how much they'd both changed—and grown—hit her with all the subtlety of a blast of dynamite. They had come a long way to get to this point. Light-years. "And," she added, "I'm depending on you to make sure everything goes right."

"God knows it had better. Because if anything happens to you or Tony . . ." He didn't finish the sentence. Instead, he pulled her to him, gave her a brief, hard kiss, and released her. Then he stroked her cheek lingeringly, gently, and let her go.

Marissa walked in to face a killer.

Evil stalked the room, tangible and deadly. The scent of fear and panic lay heavily in the air.

Marissa permitted herself one sharp glance at the bed. Tony was alive—she saw his eyes blink. Terrified, he lay curled up in a bundle of misery in the center of the bed. With another rapid glance, she scanned the room for some sort of weapon in case she needed it. She didn't see one. Then she turned her gaze to Juju Jerome, sitting in the chair by the bed, and kept it there.

A smile split his face. Ordinary, she thought. Brown hair, average height, not good-looking, not ugly. Plain. He looked like an ordinary man, if you disregarded the eyes. But the prosaic visage hid the soul of a monster.

"Well, well." Somehow, he made that simple word sound malicious. "The blonde bitch, in the flesh. Come over here. Now." He snapped his fingers and pointed to a spot in front of him, obviously enjoying his power.

Despite the frantic rate of her heartbeat, she looked him over coolly and lifted her chin. "The hell I will." Her fingers curled tightly around the small canister she held against her leg.

His smile faded. For an instant he looked taken aback. Then his brows lowered and his face darkened. "You don't learn good, do you? You shouldn't have dissed me, lady. Not now and not before. No, you shouldn't have done that. Nobody disses Juju Jerome and gets away with it."

Marissa said nothing, letting her insolent gaze speak for her.

"How does it feel, knowing the cop gave you up?" Jerome smiled again. "Thought spreadin' your—"

"Stop it!" she said sharply. Tony didn't need to hear any more. Neither did she. But Jerome wasn't through.

"What's the matter, blondie? Worried about the kid? Don't want me to spoil his tender ears, I guess. But I woulda thought he knew all about you and his old man." He started to laugh, holding his side. "Never thought Corelli would cough you up, did you?"

"But you knew he would."

His smile broadened. Slowly, he rose from the chair and walked toward her. "Blondie, I counted on it." He halted in front of her. Sure of his advantage, he held the gun loosely, not even pointing it at her—yet.

She knew he'd get around to tormenting her with it; he enjoyed the rush it gave him to have someone at his mercy. She remembered, too well, the feel of his gun sliding over her bare skin. The feel of metal against her temple. The acrid taste of fear exploding in her mouth.

Don't, she ordered herself. *Don't think about that or you won't be able to function.*

"You know the sayin', pretty lady. Blood's thicker than water. Even with a looker like you."

"I'm not his blood." Tony's voice, sounding so young, so frightened.

Marissa heard him, but she doubted Jerome had. *Say it again, Tony,* she begged silently. *Anything, just a second is all I need. Say it again.*

"Blood," Jerome said, licking his lips. "I'm gonna kill you slow, real slow. After I teach you about respect. Yeah, you're gonna learn respect real good before I'm through with you."

"Leave her alone!" Tony shouted. "I'm not his blood!"

Jerome turned his head—the perfect opening. Marissa jerked her hand up and depressed the button on the canister, aiming the pepper spray directly into his eyes.

She forgot to yell. It didn't matter, though. Jerome yelled and cursed, loud enough to be heard in the hospital morgue three floors down. Dropping the gun, he clawed wildly at his eyes, exactly as it was supposed to happen.

Jack burst into the room as Marissa scrambled for the gun. In a tangle of limbs, curses, and screams echoing loudly, he and Jerome crashed to the floor. Marissa's hand closed around the gun and she jumped quickly out of their way, reaching Tony's side in seconds. His arms went around her waist and she cradled him, murmured soothing words and thanking God that he seemed all right. Later she would check him carefully. For now it was enough to know he was alive.

Crazed with pain, still screaming, Jerome fought with the desperation of the doomed. The two men rolled, first one on top, then the other. Marissa stood frozen, silent. Tony's head moved against her and she knew he watched with her. Eons later Jack emerged on top with his hands around the other man's neck.

"Jack." She breathed his name shakily, afraid of what he'd do. "You're killing him," she said, raising her voice when he didn't appear to hear her.

"No such luck," he said, panting. But he released his hands from around Jerome's neck. "He's just unconscious. The bastard's still plenty alive." Quickly, he turned Jerome over and cuffed his hands behind his back.

Still breathing heavily, he rose and for a moment simply stared at them. The look he sent his son—no, the look he sent his son and *her*—held such huge relief and love that she felt tears prick at the back of her eyes.

"Dad?" Tony said, his voice quivering.

Jack was beside him a second later, holding him tightly. Freeing one arm, he reached out to haul her against him. Her tears gathered, spilled down her cheeks. Safe, she thought. All of them were safe.

Regaining consciousness, Jerome began to mumble, the string of obscenities he let loose growing gradually louder. Jack released them both, walked over to Jerome, and stuffed a handkerchief in his mouth.

"Shut up, scumbag," he said. "I've got to call my men," he told Marissa. "They're waiting for my signal that the operation went down as planned." He cupped her wet cheek in one hand. "Which it did, thanks to you."

Simple words, but they warmed her. Minutes later a

couple of uniformed detectives came in and removed Jerome.

When they were alone, just the three of them, Marissa told Jack that Tony had given the opening she needed.

Pride glowed in his eyes. "That's my son."

"No, I'm not," Tony said. "I'm not your son. Why didn't you tell me, Dad? Why did you lie?"

Jack looked at him, regret and pain evident in his expression. "I heard you say that when I was outside the room. That's what it's all been about, isn't it? The gang, the attitude, everything."

"It's true, isn't it? I'm not your real son. I'm adopted."

"Tony." He reached out and gripped the boy's shoulder. "You *are* my real son. As real as can be. My name is on your birth certificate. But no, you're not my biological son."

His confusion evident, Tony said, "I don't get it."

"It's a little complicated," Jack said. "A lot complicated."

"You and Mom never told me. Both of you lied to me my whole life."

"Let me try to explain. Can we talk about it? After I take care of this mess?"

"Will you tell me the truth?"

"Yeah." Jack squeezed his son's shoulder. "It's time I did. Obviously I should have done it a long time ago."

Half an hour later, after briefing Hank and dumping Jerome with him to take to the station, Jack walked back into Tony's room. Marissa sat beside the bed, talking to him quietly.

She looked up when he walked in. "Tony's going to be fine. No damage done. Physically," she added.

Mentally was another matter, Jack thought. God, why hadn't he and Elena ever told Tony? They should have realized he'd find out someday. Jack wondered how he had.

"Good," he said to her. "Jerome's on his way to jail." He turned to Tony. "I guess it's time we talked."

Marissa rose. "I'll get out of your way."

Jack stretched out a hand to her. "You can stay. You need to hear it too."

"No." She shook her head. "This is between you and your son. We'll talk later." She patted his arm. "You did great, Tony. Everyone is very proud of you."

Tony shrugged and looked embarrassed. Marissa walked out, leaving Jack alone with his son.

"How did you find out?" he asked.

"Heard Mom and Slimeball talking about it."

"And you've been mad at me ever since."

Tony looked him straight in the eye. "You lied to me. I didn't think you'd ever lie to me. Mom, well, she lies a lot. That's just the way she is. But you're not like that. At least that's what I thought. Then I found out you're just as big a liar as she is."

"You probably won't believe me now, but that's the only thing I've ever lied to you about. It's not an easy story to tell. I know that's not an excuse, but maybe you'll understand when you hear it."

Jack took a seat, trying to compose his thoughts. "You know your mother and I divorced soon after your birth. We'd been having problems for a long time. Elena and I shouldn't have married in the first place."

"Why did you, then?" Tony asked with the logic of youth.

"We thought we loved each other. But we were too different. Your mother was unhappy, even more than me. I at least had my work. She hated me being a cop, hated being a cop's wife. And I . . . wasn't very understanding. We kept growing further and further apart. So when she told me she was pregnant, I suspected that the baby wasn't mine. She insisted that it was. I found out the day you were born that you couldn't possibly be mine. Blood tests proved it."

Tony was silent, waiting for him to continue.

"About a week after you were born, Elena gave up and told me the truth, that she'd had an affair. And she told me your natural father had been killed in a car wreck early in her pregnancy. She wanted to try to make things work with us. You know that didn't happen, but we did try. For a while."

Now came the hardest part. Jack forced himself to look at Tony as he said it. "I never touched you. Never picked you up, never held you, nothing. You reminded me of what Elena had done to me, to our marriage—and you reminded me that part of it had been my fault."

"You hated me," Tony said.

"No. But I couldn't love you. Wouldn't let myself get close to you. One day, when you were three or four weeks old, your mother left you with me. She was gone for hours—and I was furious that she was forcing me to notice you. But Elena knew what she was doing." He smiled, remembering.

"You were a loud baby. Finally I couldn't stand it anymore and I picked you up. Rocked you a little bit and you stopped crying, like magic. You smiled at me. Everyone says babies don't smile that young, but you did. I can't really explain it, but I realized then that you trusted me. That it didn't matter whether you were my blood or not, you trusted me. You chose me that day—and I chose you. You were my son from that day on. In my heart, instead of just my name on your birth certificate. I've never regretted that choice a single day."

"Why didn't you tell me?" Tony burst out. "I'm not a baby anymore, you should have told me."

"Tony, your mother and I made a lot of mistakes. Most of them were damned difficult to admit to. After a few years neither of us thought about it much. You were my son as much as hers. Elena never tried to come between us. That's one thing I've always admired her for."

Slowly, Tony said, "Marissa was bugging me about seeing you and I . . . told her about it. She said blood doesn't matter, she said love's the important thing."

Jack smiled. "Marissa's smart."

"Are you going to marry her?"

"I hope so." What was he doing to do if she wouldn't?

"What if you have a kid?"

"Then you'll have a brother or sister. Think you'd baby-sit for us?"

"But—but what about me?"

It was normal, he realized, for Tony to be insecure. But it made him feel even worse. "You'll always be my son. *Nothing* will ever change that. I could have ten more children and you'd still be my firstborn. And I'll still love you."

Tony didn't speak; he seemed to be assimilating what he'd heard. Jack held his breath, praying he hadn't screwed things up beyond repair.

"Dad? Do you think you could hug me now?"

Around the lump in his throat, Jack answered. "Yeah. I think that's a real good idea."

It seemed odd, Marissa thought when she went home that afternoon, not to have someone hanging around. Odd but nice, she decided. She used the time she spent waiting for Jack to reorganize her schedule. The trauma-surgery department at FWC was about to have some major changes made. The first change would be made to Marissa's schedule—she wanted some time for a life outside the hospital.

She was in the kitchen heating water for tea when she heard the door open. Almost immediately she found herself held tight against Jack's chest. Before she could speak, he kissed her, long and hard, and then she couldn't think at all.

He drew back and took her face in his hands to stare deeply into her eyes. "I don't ever want to go through that again. Or anything like it."

She laughed shakily. "Neither do I."

"Do you know what I felt like, letting you go in there by yourself to face that maniac?"

"I know that you trusted me enough to let me do what I had to do. You couldn't have done that a few weeks ago."

He kissed her again, releasing her only when the

teakettle began shrieking. Tea in hand, she followed him into the living room.

"How did it go with Tony?"

"He's unbelievable. Maybe I don't deserve it, but I think things are going to be okay."

"You deserve every happiness that comes to you, and so does Tony."

"He told me he talked to you."

She let out a sigh. "Yes. I've never done anything harder than keeping my mouth shut about that. I wanted to tell you so badly, and I couldn't. So did Tony understand?"

"Understand?" He shook his head. "I'm not sure, but considering the story, he took it pretty well. It sounds crazy, but I'd almost forgotten that Tony wasn't my natural son. I haven't thought about it in years."

"No, it's not crazy. Knowing how much you love him, I'm not surprised you'd think that way."

"Still, it wasn't a story I ever wanted to tell him. Elena and I were stupid, I guess, to think we'd never have to." Looking at her, he said, "Now I need to tell you."

"No, you don't. Not if you don't want to."

"I want you to know, Marissa." He drew in a breath and began. "When we started having problems with our marriage, Elena had an affair. She got pregnant and tried to pass it off as mine, even though I was almost positive it wasn't. We hadn't exactly been together much, but it was remotely possible. When Tony was born, though, I found out I was right."

"But you raised him as yours. You think of him as yours. It makes no difference to you, does it? It makes no difference in how you feel about Tony." Whether

Jack thought so or not, that said a lot of good things about his character.

He shook his head again. "It doesn't make a difference now, but at first it did. Then I figured out that kids shouldn't have to pay because their parents screwed up. And I let myself love him. It was one of the best decisions I ever made."

Marissa squeezed his hand. "I love you, Jack."

He looked at her. "Enough to marry me?"

She didn't answer him directly. Staring at her mug of tea, she said, "The men in my life have never been dependable. I learned young that I was the only person I could count on. Then when I met Gil, fell in love with him, I thought maybe I was wrong. But he let me down, too, and after that I believed that the man didn't exist whom I could depend on—and who could accept my work, my life, the way it is. Then I met you, and you started to explode my theories right and left."

He smiled wryly. "But not enough for you to marry me."

"I thought I'd have to give up all my independence to marry you. I wasn't sure you could accept and respect my decisions—if you didn't agree with them."

"And now?"

She put her tea down and turned to face him. "Now I know you can. You didn't want me in that room with Jerome, you didn't want me anywhere near him, but you let me decide. You trusted me to make my own choice. And you were right there for me, just like you've always been for Tony."

"I always had you pegged for a straight talker, Doc." He grinned. "What are you trying to say?"

"I'm saying I love you and I want to marry you more than I've ever wanted anything."

Jack didn't say a word. He scooped her up in his arms and started toward the bedroom.

"What are you doing?" she asked, laughing.

"What do you think? I'm taking you to bed."

"Haven't you forgotten something?"

"What?" His smile slow and wicked, he asked, "Oh, you mean the 'I love you' part?"

"Yes, that part."

Outside her bedroom he set her down and took her in his arms. "I love you, Marissa." He sealed his words with a long, loving kiss.

Eventually she murmured, "You said you were taking me to bed."

"Changed my mind," he told her, removing her top and unfastening her bra. "We're not going to make it that far. Do you care?"

"Only if you stop," she said, and kissed him again.

THE EDITORS' CORNER

February is on the way, which can mean only one thing—it's time for Treasured Tales V! In our continuing tradition, LOVESWEPT presents four spectacular new romances inspired by age-old myths, fairy tales, and legends.

LOVESWEPT favorite Laura Taylor weaves a tapestry of love across the threads of time in **CLOUD DANCER**, LOVESWEPT #822. Smoke, flames, and a cry for help call Clayton Sloan to the rescue, but the fierce Cheyenne warrior is shocked to find himself a hero in an unknown time. Torn by fate from all that he loves, Clay is anchored only by his longing for Kelly Farrell, the brave woman who knows his secret and the torment that shadows his nights. In this breathtaking journey through history, Laura Taylor once more demonstrates her unique storytelling gifts in a moving evocation of the healing power of love.

A chance encounter turns into a passionate journey for two in **DESTINY UNKNOWN**, LOVESWEPT #823, from the talented Maris Soule. He grins at the cool beauty whose grip on a fluffy dog is about to slip, but Cody Taylor gets even more pleasure from noticing Bernadette Sanders's reaction to his down and dirty appearance. Common sense tells the sleek store executive not to get sidetracked by the glint in the maverick builder's eyes. But when he seeks her out time and time again, daring to challenge her expectations, to ignite her desire, she succumbs to her hunger for the unconventional rogue. Maris Soule demonstrates why romantic chemistry can be so deliciously explosive.

From award-winning author Suzanne Brockmann comes **OTHERWISE ENGAGED**, LOVESWEPT #824. Funny, charismatic, and one heck of a temptation, Preston Seaholm makes a wickedly sexy hero as he rescues Molly Cassidy from tumbling off the roof! The pretty widow bewitches him with a smile, unaware that the tanned sun god is Sunrise Key's mysterious tycoon—and one of the most eligible bachelors in the country. He needs her help to fend off unwanted advances, but once he's persuaded her to play along at pretending they're engaged, he finds himself helplessly surrendering to her temptation. As fast-paced and touching as it is sensual, this is another winner from Suzanne Brockmann.

Last but not least, Kathy Lynn Emerson offers a hero who learns to **LOVE THY NEIGHBOR**, LOVESWEPT #825. The moment she drives up in a flame-red Mustang to claim the crumbling house next door, Marshall Austin knows he was right. Linnea Bryan is bewitching, a fascinating puzzle who can easily hold him spellbound—but she is also the daughter of the woman who destroyed his parents' marriage. So he launches his campaign to send her packing. But even as he insists he wants her out of town by nightfall, his heart is really saying he wants her all night long. Kathy Lynn Emerson draws the battle lines, then lets the seduction begin in her LOVESWEPT debut!

Happy reading!

With warmest wishes,

Beth de Guzman   Shauna Summers

Senior Editor   Editor

P.S. Watch for these Bantam women's fiction titles coming in February: Available for the first time in paperback is the *New York Times* bestseller **GUILTY AS SIN** by the new master of suspense, Tami Hoag. Jane Feather, author of the nationally bestselling *VICE* and *VALENTINE*, is set to thrill romance lovers once again with **THE DIAMOND SLIPPER,** a tale of passion and intrigue involving a forced bride, a reluctant hero, and a jeweled charm. And finally, from Michelle Martin comes **STOLEN HEARTS,** a contemporary romance in the tradition of Jayne Ann Krentz in which an ex–jewel thief pulls the con of her life, but one man is determined to catch her—and never let her get away. Don't miss the previews of these exceptional novels in next month's LOVE-SWEPTs. And immediately following this page, sneak a peek at the Bantam women's fiction titles on sale *now*!

For current information on Bantam's women's fiction, visit our new web site, *Isn't It Romantic,* at the following address: **http://www.bdd.com/romance**

Don't miss these terrific novels
by your favorite Bantam authors

On sale in December:

HAWK O'TOOLE'S HOSTAGE
by Sandra Brown

THE UGLY DUCKLING
by Iris Johansen

WICKED
by Susan Johnson

HEART OF THE FALCON
by Suzanne Robinson

Sandra Brown

Her heady blend of passion, humor, and high-voltage romantic suspense has made her one of the most beloved writers in America. Now the author of more than two dozen New York Times bestsellers weaves a thrilling tale of a woman who finds herself at the mercy of a handsome stranger—and the treacherous feelings only he can arouse. . . .

HAWK O'TOOLE'S HOSTAGE

A classic Bantam romance available in hardcover for the first time in December 1996

To Hawk O'Toole, she was a pawn in a desperate gamble to help his people. To Miranda Price, he was a stranger who'd done the unthinkable: kidnapped her and her young son from a train full of sight-seeing vacationers. Now held hostage on a distant reservation for reasons she cannot at first fathom, Miranda finds herself battling a captor who is by turns harsh and tender, mysteriously aloof, and dangerously seductive.

Hawk assumed that Miranda, the beautiful ex-wife of Representative Price, would be as selfish and immoral as the tabloids suggested. Instead, she seems genuinely afraid for her son's life—and willing to risk her own to keep his safe. But, committed to a fight he didn't start, Hawk knows he can't afford to feel anything but contempt for his prisoner. To force the government to reopen the Lone Puma Mine, he must keep Miranda at arm's length, to remember that she is his enemy—even when she ignites his deepest desires.

Slowly, Miranda begins to learn what drives this brooding, solitary man, to discover the truth about his tragic past. But it will take a shocking revelation to finally force her to face her own past and the woman she's become . . . and to ask herself: Is it freedom she really wants . . . or the chance to stay with Hawk forever?

"Only Iris Johansen can so magically mix a love story with hair-raising adventure and suspense. Don't miss this page-turner."—Catherine Coulter

THE UGLY DUCKLING

by *New York Times* bestselling author

Iris Johansen

now available in paperback

Plain, soft-spoken Nell Calder isn't the type of woman to inspire envy, lust—or murderous passion. Until one night when the unimaginable happens, and her life, her dreams, her future, are shattered by a brutal attack. Though badly hurt, she emerges from the nightmare a woman transformed, with an exquisitely beautiful face and strong, lithe body. While Nicholas Tanek, a mysterious stranger who compels both fear and fascination, gives her a reason to go on living. But divulging the identity of her assailant to Nell might just turn out to be the biggest mistake of Tanek's life. For he will soon find his carefully laid plans jeopardized by Nell's daring to strike out on her own.

He had come for nothing, Nicholas thought in disgust as he gazed down at the surf crashing on the rocks below. No one would want to kill Nell Calder. She was no more likely to be connected with Gardeaux than that big-eyed elf she was now lavishing with French pastry and adoration.

If there was a target here, it was probably Kavinski. As head of an emerging Russian state, he had the power to be either a cash cow or extremely troublesome to Gardeaux. Nell Calder wouldn't be considered troublesome to anyone. He had known the answers to all the questions he had asked her, but he had wanted to see her reactions. He had been watching her all evening, and it was clear she was a nice, shy woman, totally out of her depth even with those fairly innocuous sharks downstairs. He couldn't imagine her having enough influence to warrant bribery, and she would never have been able to deal one-on-one with Gardeaux.

Unless she was more than she appeared. Possibly. She seemed as meek as a lamb, but she'd had the guts to toss him out of her daughter's room.

Everyone fought back if the battle was important enough. And it was important for Nell Calder not to share her daughter with him. No, the list must mean something else. When he went back downstairs, he would stay close to Kavinski.

> "Here we go up, up, up
> High in the sky so blue.
> Here we go down, down, down
> Touching the rose so red."

She was singing to the kid. He had always liked lullabies. There was a reassuring continuity about them that had been missing in his own life. Since the dawn of time, mothers had sung to their children, and they would probably still be singing to them a thousand years from then.

The song ended with a low chuckle and a murmur he couldn't hear.

She came out of the bedroom and closed the door

a few minutes later. She was flushed and glowing with an expression as soft as melted butter.

"I've never heard that lullaby before," he said.

She looked startled, as if she'd forgotten he was still there. "It's very old. My grandmother used to sing it to me."

"Is your daughter asleep?"

"No, but she will be soon. I started the music box for her again. By the time it finishes, she usually nods off."

"She's a beautiful child."

"Yes." A luminous smile turned her plain face radiant once more. "Yes, she is."

He stared at her, intrigued. He found he wanted to keep that smile on her face. "And bright?"

"Sometimes too bright. Her imagination can be troublesome. But she's always reasonable and you can talk to—" She broke off and her eagerness faded. "But this can't interest you. I forgot the tray. I'll go back for it."

"Don't bother. You'll disturb Jill. The maid can pick it up in the morning."

She gave him a level glance. "That's what I told you."

He smiled. "But then I didn't want to listen. Now it makes perfect sense to me."

"Because it's what you want to do."

"Exactly."

"I have to go back too. I haven't met Kavinski yet." She moved toward the door.

"Wait. I think you'll want to remove that chocolate from your gown first."

"Damn." She frowned as she looked down at the stain on the skirt. "I forgot." She turned toward the bathroom and said dryly, "Go on. I assure you I don't need your help with this problem."

He hesitated.

She glanced at him pointedly over her shoulder.

He had no excuse for staying, not that that small fact would have deterred him.

But he also had no reason. He had lived by his wits too long not to trust his instincts, and this woman wasn't a target of any sort. He should be watching Kavinski.

He turned toward the door. "I'll tell the maid you're ready for her to come back."

"Thank you, that's very kind of you," she said automatically as she disappeared into the bathroom.

Good manners obviously instilled from childhood. Loyalty. Gentleness. A nice woman whose world was centered on that sweet kid. He had definitely drawn a blank.

The maid wasn't waiting in the hallway. He'd have to send up one of the servants from downstairs.

He moved quickly through the corridors and started down the staircase.

Shots.

Coming from the ballroom.

Christ.

He tore down the stairs.

WICKED

by Susan Johnson

"An exceptional writer."—*Affaire de Coeur*

Serena Blythe's plans to escape a life of servitude had gone terribly awry. So she took the only course left to her. She sneaked aboard a sleek yacht about to set sail—and found herself face-to-face with a dangerous sensual stranger. Beau St. Jules, the Earl of Rochefort, had long surpassed his father's notoriety as a libertine. Less well known was his role as intelligence-gatherer for England. Yet even on a mission to seek vital war information, he couldn't resist practicing his well-polished seduction on the beautiful, disarmingly innocent stowaway. And in the weeks to come, with battles breaking out on the Continent and Serena's life in peril, St. Jules would risk everything to rescue the one woman who'd finally captured his heart.

"Your life sounds idyllic. Unlike mine of late," Serena said with a fleeting grimace. "But I intend to change that."

Frantic warning bells went off in Beau's consciousness. Had she *deliberately* come on board? Were her designing relatives even now in hot pursuit? Or were they explaining the ruinous details to his father instead? "How exactly," he softly inquired, his dark eyes wary, "do you plan on facilitating those changes?"

"Don't be alarmed," she said, suddenly grinning. "I have no designs on you."

He laughed, his good spirits instantly restored. "Candid women have always appealed to me."

"While men with yachts are out of my league." Her smile was dazzling. "But why don't you deal us another hand," she cheerfully said, "and I'll see what I can do about mending my fortunes."

She was either completely ingenuous or the most skillful coquette. But he had more than enough money to indulge her, and she amused him immensely.

He dealt the cards.

And when the beefsteaks arrived sometime later, the cards were put away and they both tucked into the succulent meat with gusto.

She ate with a quiet intensity, absorbed in the food and the act of eating. It made him consider his casual acceptance of all the privileges in his life with a new regard. But only briefly, because he was very young, very wealthy, too handsome for complete humility, and beset by intense carnal impulses that were profoundly immune to principle.

He'd simply offer her a liberal settlement when the *Siren* docked in Naples, he thought, discarding any further moral scruples.

He glanced at the clock.

Three-thirty.

They'd be making love in the golden light of dawn . . . or sooner perhaps, he thought with a faint smile, reaching across the small table to refill her wineglass.

"This must be heaven or very near . . ." Serena murmured, looking up from cutting another portion of beefsteak. "I can't thank you enough."

"Remy deserves all the credit."

"You're very disarming. And kind."

"You're very beautiful, Miss Blythe. And a damned good card player."

"Papa practiced with me. He was an accomplished player when he wasn't drinking."

"Have you thought of making your fortune in the gaming rooms instead of wasting your time as an underpaid governess?"

"No," she softly said, her gaze direct.

"Forgive me. I meant no rudeness. But the demi-monde is not without its charm."

"I'm sure it is for a man," she said, taking a squarely cut piece of steak off her fork with perfect white teeth. "However, I'm going to art school in Florence," she went on, beginning to chew. "And I shall make my living painting."

"Painting what?"

She chewed a moment more, savoring the flavors, then swallowed. "Portraits, of course. Where the money is. I shall be flattering in the extreme. I'm very good, you know."

"I'm sure you are." And he intended to find out how good she was in other ways as well. "Why don't I give you your first commission?" He'd stopped eating but he'd not stopped drinking, and he gazed at her over the rim of his wineglass.

"I don't have my paints. They're on the *Betty Lee* with my luggage."

"We could put ashore in Portugal and buy you some. How much do you charge?"

Her gaze shifted from her plate. "Nothing for you. You've been generous in the extreme. I'd be honored to paint you"—she paused and smiled—"whoever you are."

"Beau St. Jules."

"*The* Beau St. Jules?" She put her flatware down and openly studied him. "The darling of the broad-sheets . . . London's premier rake who's outsinned his father, The Saint?" A note of teasing had entered her voice, a familiar, intimate reflection occasioned by the numerous glasses of wine she'd drunk. "Should I be alarmed?"

He shook his head, amusement in his eyes. "I'm very ordinary," he modestly said, this man who stood stud to all the London beauties. "You needn't be alarmed."

He wasn't ordinary, of course, not in any way. He was the gold standard, she didn't doubt, by which male beauty was judged. His perfect features and artfully cropped black hair reminded her of classic Greek sculpture; his overt masculinity, however, was much less the refined cultural ideal. He was startlingly male.

"Aren't rakes older? You're very young," she declared. And gorgeous as a young god, she decided, although the cachet of his notorious reputation probably wasn't based on his beauty alone. He was very charming.

He shrugged at her comment on his age. He'd begun his carnal amusements very young he could have said, but, circumspect, asked instead, "How old are *you?*" His smile was warm, personal. "Out in the world on your own?"

"Twenty-three." Her voice held a small defiance; a single lady of three and twenty was deemed a spinster in any society.

"A very nice age," he pleasantly noted, his dark eyes lazily half-lidded. "Do you like floating islands?"

She looked at him blankly.

"The dessert."

"Oh, yes, of course." She smiled. "I should save room then."

By all means, he licentiously thought, nodding a smiling approval, filling their wineglasses once more. *Save room for me—because I'm coming in. . . .*

Blazing with romance, intrigue, and the splendor of
ancient Egypt

HEART OF
THE FALCON

The bestselling

Suzanne Robinson
at her finest

*All her life, raven-haired Anqet had basked in the tran-
quillity of Nefer . . . until the day her father died and
her uncle descended upon the estate, hungry for her land,
hungry for her. Desperate to escape his cruel obsession, she
fled. But now, masquerading as a commoner in the mag-
nificent city of Thebes, Anqet faces a new danger. Mysterious and seductive, Count Seth seems to be a loyal soldier to
the pharaoh. Yet soon Anqet will find that he's drawn her
back into a web of treachery and desire, where one false
move could end her life and his fiery passion could brand
her soul.*

    Anqet waited for the procession to pass. She had
asked for directions to the Street of the Scarab. If she
was correct, this alley would lead directly to her goal.
She followed the dusty, shaded path between win-
dowless buildings, eager to reach the house of Lady
Gasantra before dark. She hadn't eaten since leaving
her barber companion and his family earlier in the
afternoon, and her stomach rumbled noisily. She

hoped Tamit would remember her. They hadn't seen each other for several years.

The alley twisted back and forth several times, but Anqet at last saw the intersection with the Street of the Scarab. Intent upon reaching the end of her journey, she ran into the road, into the path of an oncoming chariot.

There was a shout, then the screams of outraged horses as the driver of the chariot hauled his animals back. Anqet ducked to the ground beneath pawing hooves. Swerving, the vehicle skidded and tipped. The horses reared and stamped, showering stones and dust over Anqet.

From behind the bronze-plated chariot came a stream of oaths. Someone pounced on Anqet from the vehicle, hauling her to her feet by her hair, and shaking her roughly.

"You little gutter-frog! I ought to whip you for dashing about like a demented antelope. You could have caused one of my horses to break a leg."

Anqet's head rattled on her shoulders. Surprised, she bore with this treatment for a few moments before stamping on a sandaled foot. There was a yelp. The shaking stopped, but now two strong hands gripped her wrists. Silence reigned while her attacker recovered from his pain, then a new string of obscenities rained upon her. The retort she thought up never passed her lips, for when she raised her eyes to those of the charioteer, she forgot her words.

Eyes of deep green, the color of the leaves of a water lily. Eyes weren't supposed to be green. Eyes were brown, or black, and they didn't glaze with the molten fury of the Lake of Fire in the *Book of the Dead*. Anqet stared into those pools of malachite until, at a call behind her, they shifted to look over her head.

"Count Seth! My lord, are you injured?"

"No, Dega. See to the horses while I deal with this, this . . ."

Anqet stared up at the count while he spoke to his servant. He was unlike any man she had ever seen. Tall, slender, with lean, catlike muscles, he had wide shoulders that were in perfect proportion to his flat torso and long legs. He wore a short soldier's kilt belted around his hips. A bronze corselet stretched tight across his wide chest; leather bands protected his wrists and accentuated elegant, long-fingered hands that gripped Anqet in a numbing hold. Anqet gazed back at Count Seth and noted the strange auburn tint of the silky hair that fell almost to his shoulders. He was beautiful. Exotic and beautiful, and wildly furious.

Count Seth snarled at her. "You're fortunate my team wasn't hurt, or I'd take their cost out on your hide."

Anqet's temper flared. She forgot that she was supposed to be a humble commoner. Her chin came up, her voice raised in command.

"Release me at once."

Shock made Count Seth obey the order. No woman spoke to him thus. For the first time, he really looked at the girl before him. She faced him squarely and met his gaze, not with the humility or appreciation he was used to, but with the anger of an equal.

Bareka! What an uncommonly beautiful commoner. Where in the Two Lands had she gotten those fragile features? Her face was enchanting. High-arched brows curved over enormous black eyes that glittered with highlights of brown and inspected him as if he were a stray dog.

Seth let his eyes rest for a moment on her lips. To watch them move made him want to lick them. He appraised the fullness of her breasts and the length of her legs. To his chagrin, he felt a wave of desire pulse through his veins and settle demandingly in his groin.

Curse the girl. She had stirred him past control. Well, he was never one to neglect an opportunity. What else could be expected of a barbarian half-breed?

Seth moved with the swiftness of an attacking lion, pulling the girl to him. She fit perfectly against his body. Her soft flesh made him want to thrust his hips against her, right in the middle of the street. He cursed as she squirmed against him in a futile effort to escape and further tortured his barely leashed senses.

"Release me!"

Seth uttered a light, mocking laugh. "Compose yourself, my sweet. Surely you won't mind repaying me for my inconvenience?"

On sale in January:

GUILTY AS SIN
by Tami Hoag

THE DIAMOND SLIPPER
by Jane Feather

STOLEN HEARTS
by Michelle Martin

DON'T MISS THESE FABULOUS BANTAM WOMEN'S FICTION TITLES

On Sale in December

HAWK O'TOOLE'S HOSTAGE

by *New York Times* megaselling phenomenon SANDRA BROWN
Another heady blend of the passion, humor, and high-voltage romantic suspense that has made Sandra Brown one of the most beloved writers in America. Now in hardcover for the first time, this is the thrilling tale of a woman who finds herself at the mercy of a handsome stranger—and the treacherous feelings only he can arouse. ____ 10448-9 $17.95/$24.95

"A spectacular tale of revenge, betrayal and survival." —*Publishers Weekly*
From *New York Times* bestselling author IRIS JOHANSEN comes

THE UGLY DUCKLING in paperback ____ 56991-0 $5.99/$7.99

"Susan Johnson is queen of erotic romance." —*Romantic Times*

WICKED

by bestselling author SUSAN JOHNSON
No one sizzles like Susan Johnson, and she burns up the pages in *Wicked*. Governess Serena Blythe had been saving for years to escape to Florence. Despite her well-laid plans, there were two developments she couldn't foresee: that she would end up a stowaway—and that the ship's master would be an expert at seduction. ____ 57214-8 $5.99/$7.99

From the bestselling author of *The Engagement* SUZANNE ROBINSON

HEART OF THE FALCON

Rich with the pageantry of ancient Egypt and aflame with the unforgettable romance of a woman who has lost everything only to find the man who will brand her soul, this is the unforgettable Suzanne Robinson at her finest. ____ 28138-0 $5.50/$7.50

Ask for these books at your local bookstore or use this page to order.

Please send me the books I have checked above. I am enclosing $____ (add $2.50 to cover postage and handling). Send check or money order, no cash or C.O.D.'s, please.

Name _____

Address _____

City/State/Zip _____

Send order to: Bantam Books, Dept. FN158, 2451 S. Wolf Rd., Des Plaines, IL 60018
Allow four to six weeks for delivery.
Prices and availability subject to change without notice. FN 158 12/96

DON'T MISS THESE FABULOUS
BANTAM WOMEN'S FICTION TITLES

On Sale in January

GUILTY AS SIN
by TAMI HOAG

The terror that began in *Night Sins* continues in this spine-chilling *New York Times* bestseller. Now available in paperback.

_____ 56452-8 $6.50/$8.99

THE DIAMOND SLIPPER
by the incomparable JANE FEATHER
nationally bestselling author of Vice *and* Vanity

With her delightful wit and gift for storytelling, Jane Feather brings to life the breathtaking tale of a determined heroine, a sinister lover, and the intrigue of a mysterious past in this, the first book of her new Charm Bracelet trilogy.

_____ 57523-6 $5.99/$7.99

From the fresh new voice of MICHELLE MARTIN
STOLEN HEARTS

This sparkling romance in the tradition of Jayne Ann Krentz tells the tale of an ex-jewel thief who pulls the con of her life and the one man who is determined to catch her—and never let her get away.

_____ 57648-8 $5.50/$7.50

Ask for these books at your local bookstore or use this page to order.

Please send me the books I have checked above. I am enclosing $_____ (add $2.50 to cover postage and handling). Send check or money order, no cash or C.O.D.'s, please.

Name _____

Address _____

City/State/Zip _____

Send order to: Bantam Books, Dept. FN159, 2451 S. Wolf Rd., Des Plaines, IL 60018.
Allow four to six weeks for delivery.

Prices and availability subject to change without notice.   FN 159 1/97